From the Dark Domain

From the Dark Domain

Novel Number One in the *Luke Thomas* Series

KEITH POTTER

RESOURCE *Publications* · Eugene, Oregon

FROM THE DARK DOMAIN

Resource Publications
An Imprint of Wipf and Stock Publishers
199 W. 8th Ave., Suite 3
Eugene, OR 97401

www.wipfandstock.com

PAPERBACK ISBN: 978-1-7252-7005-3
HARDCOVER ISBN: 978-1-7252-7006-0
EBOOK ISBN: 978-1-7252-7007-7

Manufactured in the U.S.A.   10/02/20

To the late Reverend Dr. Gary Wells.
A true pastor, a great professor and a credible man.
I borrowed your voice
and remember your words.

Up from the grave he arose
with a mighty triumph o'er his foes
He arose a victor from the dark domain
And he lives forever
with his saints to reign
he arose
he arose
hallelujah
Christ arose

Contents

BOOK THREE

CONCLUSION

Acknowledgments

FICTION IS SO DIFFERENT than non-fiction. After laying bare my first written gurgitation of imagination to a friend, his response set me back months. "I feel like I've seen you in your underwear." After some recovery, I committed to the brave work of exposing.

To that end, I want to thank Nancy Commins for early manuscript efforts and my new friends at Wipf and Stock for their final touches. Sally Bryant and Jackie Hester believed in this enterprise while others urged me to "stick to the day job." Ronnie and Karen Lott, along with Dennis and Stacey Barsema, led me to Rwanda in concert with our partners at Opportunity International, where I fell in love with the people and place. An extraordinary guide, Bishop John, showed us the best in Rwandan education and orphan care. Two books offered keen preparation for telling the awful story of genocide: *Shake Hands with the Devil: The Failure of Humanity in Rwanda*, by Lt. Gen. Romæo Dallaire, and *Left to Tell: Discovering God Amidst the Rwandan Holocaust*, by Immaculée Ilibagiza.

Speaking of exposing, Book Two has some overtly sexual parts, especially for a work that will have a faith-inclined readership. For the courage and care required, I did a deep read of *Redeeming Love*, by Francine Rivers. While Rivers has earned the right, far more than I, to push the boundaries of Christian writing, I am drafting on her model of honest (if at times voyeuristic) prose that leads to a more believable premise. Please try not to be offended, but rather sympathetic to the force of human sexuality, as well as the healing required in the lives of the characters—as in many of our own. The narrative also includes a critique of the Church, especially in its extremes on the far right and left. With respect to all, the chief character drafts on his own self-discovery to find his voice about the whole work and person of Jesus. Again, the intention is not to offend, but certainly to chide us all toward a lively communion in the middle space between extremes, where the best work gets done.

I'm grateful to my kind and courageous wife, Sue, and children Kristen (and Joe), Erin, and Luke for granting the space and encouragement to create. Friends at Saratoga Federated Church often asked how this project and others have been progressing. Northwest Christian College (now Bushnell University) taught skills and shaped my worldview as a student, and offers a playground for this season of passionate service.

It's worth noting that all characters in this book are fictitious constructs and amalgamations born from my imagination. Only bits and pieces of each episode are the products of walking through this beautiful but imperfect life with brave, broken people like me.

Prologue

ONE SMALL ROOM CONTAINS his entire world. Two beds lie side by side with barely enough space for a spartan chair between. Arthur Gilliam's roommate sleeps restlessly near the window surrounded by crayon drawings and laughing snapshots of great grandchildren. He mutters now and then, dreaming of younger days or missed adventures, his left knee jerking under a sheet and one thin blanket. Gaunt and unshaven, he still emanates life—mostly past, but still present, and he looks to live another five years before dying with a toothless grin.

But the bed toward the door hardly strains under the still more emaciated figure before me. This subject of my interest has teeth, but they only serve to fill out his features. Arthur won't be smiling or eating or talking again this side of God's banqueting hall. A series of strokes has taken his capacities for normal living and buried them out of reach, leaving him alive in a tired shell. His eyes stare at the ceiling. If they see me or anything else in the room, they offer no warmth or welcome. Rather, Arthur's eyes scan slightly over the textured sheetrock of the ceiling as if a story is scrolling across the institutional Navajo White paint. Arthur Gilliam is rapt in the final chapters, straining to reach the resolution of a plot so diabolical that he senses no one and nothing else in his paltry environment.

No pictures adorn Arthur's wall. A worn Bible sits on the rolling table that lines the left rail of his bed. But not one card or flower or keepsake decorates his space, save the smell of urine wafting from the sheets; the only real evidence of function beyond those eyes panning from his left to right.

And his chart, on a clipboard in a rack screwed to the footboard of his bed.

Two nurses come and then go, after hassling with tubes and uttering reassurances to their prone patients. Both Filipino, the women speak to their patients in an unknown and probably unheard language, but the tone is familiar, like mothers cooing at infants as if these grown and ingrown men have receded into sucklings. To their credit, I imagine that it helps the caregiver to change gnarly diapers and wipe wrinkled remains if she can imagine the limp host to be a helpless child. It all seems insulting to me. Still, these are steady and generous women doing a job I don't covet; a job they'll still be attending to long after I leave the room gasping for fresh air and many more decades before I'm the one lying here.

My job as a pastor sends me into these settings—never my preference—and then I leave. My spiritual comfort is a fleeting offering. I lob a lofty "be warm and well fed" and then abdicate the crappy tasks to others. Perhaps my day will come to provide steady presence for someone I love more than Arthur. Until then, I stay and pray as long as I can handle the stench and then walk out coughing and hoping the residue won't stick to me as I go on to my next appointment with people who would rather I not smell like a carpet in a house overfull with cats.

My habit is to return to the charms of office and church and the ordinary trials of helping people cope with life and integrate faith.

All good, of course, but the ladies in this room are living Jesus. They care for men who, whatever they might have been, have now become "the least of these."

There's more in the rack at Arthur's feet. There are three manila envelopes tight with content. And there's an army-green folder, which I dare to open. I find clean and clear documents recording Arthur's wishes not to be extraordinarily resuscitated or artificially sustained—at least not beyond the tubes that feed directly under his bedclothes to his beleaguered body.

Feeling ashamed for snooping, I step to the head of the bed and put an arm over Arthur onto the opposite rail until I can look directly into his eyes. They offer no indication of awareness, but I've been told many times that patients like Arthur can still hear.

"Arthur, I'm Luke Thomas. I'm the District Pastor. I've been told that you've been . . . you are a pastor, too. And it seems that you've named the District as your executor. I wanted to meet you. Maybe I can visit now and then; even read some scripture and pray with you."

My informants told me that Arthur Gilliam has pastored churches in the Pacific Northwest. From there he went to Africa before coming back to interim pastorates in small American churches. Then came the first strokes, a retirement center in San Diego and, finally, this skilled nursing facility. No known family. His parishioners are continents and decades away. It appears that I'm all he has. Well, he has those dear ladies. No one else to my knowledge knows his story.

I fidget and prepare to make my exit. But then I think that those manila envelopes are for my eyes as much as anyone's. I grab the first and slide the thick stack of typed pages from its sepulcher.

Did I imagine that Arthur flinched or shuddered? The first page was a cover letter.

February, 2002

Dear Donnie,
It's so hard to be quiet when quiet is all I can be. I know that I was too quiet when other options stood ready. But alas, this recent stroke has taken speech captive, and I fear that another will soon steal my right side as others robbed me of my left.

There's so much I'd like to tell you. Please know, first of all, that I love you. We've disappointed each other through the years, you and I. Still, you are my son, and I've always treasured the privilege of being your father. Nothing could change my deep affection for you.

Second, you must know that your mother loved you. She had difficulty saying it and perhaps still more difficulty proving it. But rest in this—in the early years, she found more joy in holding you and feeding you and, yes, even singing to you than you could imagine.

Her life took a turn. Our lives came undone. We all suffered some. Still, you were always in her heart, Donnie. And mine.

I fear being a burden. I long to be more independent. I wish to leave you a legacy better than the meager bag of regrets and betrayals that you've had to carry on your way.

So, I leave you this story. Not a fortune or an estate, but a trust. You and perhaps others can measure its worth. I only hope that it peels away the dark draperies of a bleak childhood and affords light into the room of your memories.

Whether you need to know it, I need to tell it—that I am not an entirely ruined man. Please read all three books, and in order, or else you'll never know me the way I crave your knowing. I did not live well with the thought of your lingering disrespect. I blanch at the notion of dying with it.

Oh, this language sounds so stiff and angular. I always hoped to learn another way of speaking and being—more hip or cool, as you might have said. But I couldn't change then and don't have the energy now.

So please forgive the tone and diction. And, my son, please forgive me.

For I will always be one father who loves you, less and worse than the First and Best. But still I love you for the rest of this life and forever into the next.

Dad

"You've written your life story, Arthur?"
No response.
"And you have a son? Is he alive? Does he live anywhere around here?"
Stillness.
I check my iCalendar. No pressing commitments. I plop down in the chair and forge through the stench until it's forgotten and replaced by other influences. I glance once more into the author's passive face and then walk into his world.

BOOK ONE

Chapter 1

EUGENE, OREGON, WAS A fairyland of possibility, with forests and rivers running between buttes that stood like the king's guard over the ever-growing city of bricks and mortar and mortarboards that is the University.

There, in our small house built for millers, we made a life under the influence of the unique and constant odor of pulp mills. Weyerhaeuser and Georgia Pacific and International Paper hummed with industry along the roaring Willamette and the eddies ebbed and banks cascaded in logs waiting to be cut or floated or hauled or chipped or shipped. Finally, those felled trees became houses or paper or milk cartons in homes all over the west, and even in Asia.

And in the middle of it all, standing taller in my mind even than the ivy walls of MacArthur Court or the grandstands of Hayward Field or the pillared halls of learning, stood majestic Village Church of Eugene. With the notion that all Christians can lay aside differences, Village church gathered diverse comers under a frescoed dome that might have been suspended in the heavens of that place by Michelangelo himself.

My family walked from our tiny home near Coburg Road and out from under the shadow of the smokestacks until we could almost baptize away the stench of pulp with the rumbling rivers of the pipe organ. There I met the Lord in the dark pews and within the tall arched windows and beneath that dome that spoke heavily about the mighty hand of God.

My parents were God-fearing people, though my mother feared him not enough, or she would have held her tongue more. And my father carried a steady fear of God's recompense for deeds done in darkness past. His greater dread was of his wife, who punished him regularly for some unmentionable sin and uttered the name Sally James like a cussword. This left me to surmise that my father, once a professor of literature and composition, had involved himself with a woman—or possibly a girl—in a way that defamed him and cast him into the new vocation of mill hand.

Still, he trained me in letters and harped gently on my diction until I spoke a dialect more like the son of nobility and less like the son of a miller. He didn't want his life for me.

Nor did my mother, though she wanted it still less for herself. She wept often and wailed away at her situation until Father and I mastered every form of appeasement and avoidance known to man.

Then, of course, she grieved on more than one count.

My sister.

On a day of blue skies and green trees that the Pacific Northwest produces like gems rare and brilliant, my sister Angela coaxed me to the docks. Longshoremen heaved their loads and smoked cigarettes and swore colorful oaths while we sneaked and peeked around crates. Then on to the chipper that sprayed wood bits into a pile the size of nearby Skinner's Butte. Finally, ever so finally, we skirted the banks until we found a gigantic but disconnected raft of Douglas Fir drifting in the shallows.

Forever fun and bold, Angie's favorite game was Huck Finn and Tom Sawyer. She played Huck, of course. I played Tom and we imagined that Jim rode the raft with us along the great Missouri. We refined our *southun'* accents and sailed to dreamy islands of freedom.

The lurking dangers were everywhere, greater than our imagined foes. According to our script, Injun Joe lurked nearby and menacing steamboats plowed toward our raft. In the real world, those disconnected logs swayed and rolled and bumped each other with forces stronger than their gentle movements revealed.

We'd been warned. Giant men had chased us off those logs more than twice. But Angie believed in herself, and I believed in Angie, so sure-footed and adept at skipping over roiling terrain until the threat no longer plagued our revelry.

In one cruel instant, a log shifted and rolled heartless and relentless, capturing Angie's foot and crushing her ankle. The current pushed the logs tight against each other, or else hidden influences above or below destined my sister for a short life. Suddenly, the logs released her pinned leg and separated. Just as quickly, they spun inward so that my grimacing older sister splashed into the brown waters. So quickly, like a monster of lore, the mouth closed again with Angie beneath and swallowed her up.

I pulled and pushed and kicked against the beast, putting my own life into every kind of peril. Angie must have swum and squeezed into each potential opening from below while I screamed and bawled for help from God and all humanity. Both arrived too late and divers hauled Angie's body from the waters after three agonizing hours.

Father came and held me, weeping for his only daughter, lending me solace and absolution and grieving in gentle ways. Mother arrived, screaming recriminations, barely shedding a tear, but grieving straight out of her bile duct. Some people, on stubbing a toe or hitting a thumb with a hammer, simply cry "ouch!" and see no need to punish the offending table or hammer or nail. Hurt means pain without rage. Others can't stub or crush without swearing, blaming and punishing. Anger is so near the surface that it blasts out at the moment of insult and settles into an ooze of sting and stain.

Father said "ouch" with heart and purpose and allowed me to join in.

Mother said so much more and meant it. I would suffer her toxic grief all my life. I might as well have shot Angela in the face out of malice. And my poor father might as well have loaded the gun, since her perception of his neglect would sentence him to a lifetime of scorn.

They slept separately. We ate quietly. Father worked laboriously and I played long hours of baseball. I delivered the Oregonian early in the morning and collected fees door to door long into the evenings to steer clear of the river of accusation flowing like a dark brown slough through our house.

I loved Angie. I missed Angie. I don't blame anyone, though the aftermath is hardly simple math. It leaves me perplexed by the notion that anyone would throw away all that remains of this life simply because another one, however dear, has been lost.

Mother ended our torment by dying of pancreatic cancer when I was sixteen. Her bitterness settled into a little known but utterly critical host organ and the punishment intended for us was visited upon her. Not that I blame God for that loss. It was a reprieve for all of us. God rest her soul.

Chapter 2

CHURCH RESCUED ME. I suppose I should say that Christ saved me. But before my sensitivities developed for God and the gospel, the church became true sanctuary.

First came the building. I know that I shouldn't have an edifice complex. Surely God does not dwell in buildings made by human hands. All the world is God's sanctuary. Still, those brown pews felt forever and friendly and the dark eyes of the bell tower uttered a quiet welcome as they danced with peals of a muscular but benevolent God.

The baseball park worked a similar grace. Manicured lawns of deep green in summer and yellow in winter stroked some barren part of my internal terrain, along with the urine smell of the dugouts and the strewn candy wrappers from the snack shack that reminded me that I traversed the world with others not immune from messes. This carpeted expanse felt homier than the living room of my childhood and even became that living room.

While the church was my family room. On the inside, the majestic pillars and stained glass melded me into a fairy tale of noble persuasions winning wars over evil. In that room, people spoke gently. Pastors preached themes of peaceful purpose. The organ rumbled my innards and the choir embodied a level of cooperation that defied the tensions and isolation of life in our home. The gentle blend of a brief choral introit ushered me into a space so removed from strain that I realized early how unlike any other child or teen I truly was—I loved to be in church.

Sunday school held less sway. While peers whimpered and waggled like puppies around female teachers, I felt annoyed by their disinterest and curious about the lessons. I preferred the adults and grownup worship, and while Dr. Everson's sermons perplexed me at times, they did not bore me. So used to finding solitude and keeping my own counsel in order to avoid my raging mother, I found the quiet of worship familiar and the solicitations of the pastor welcome.

At thirteen, I began ushering amused and delighted parishioners. At fourteen, I joined my father in the choir, though still more alto than tenor. At seventeen, I became part-time custodian. The quiet hours dusting pews and cleaning bathrooms fostered healing from the strange manner of grieving that comes with the death of a parent who has not loved well. The loss is over a relationship that never was. The guilt over my sense of relief at her death made me feel monstrous.

Then father died.

Not out of grief for his wife, for he'd grieved the loss of Mother years before at the loss of his daughter. He died of a heart attack and liver issues, aided by years of smoking and heavy late-night drinking, when he'd anesthetize himself in an easy chair and wake up in the early hours, undress for a short, lonely sleep in a twin bed and then rise to the alarm and stagger to work again. For a man of letters and words, perhaps with artistic impulses and even books backed up like logs in a flume, his life must have felt desperate. Choir rehearsals and Sunday mornings seemed to be his only real pleasures.

And me. He did love me.

Those few years in the choir together were our best moments. He'd sober up, drink some mouthwash and wear the same clean shirt each Wednesday night.

"You ready to make a joyful noise?" he'd ask, as we climbed into our beat-up Rambler.

"Noise, anyway," I'd say every time, and he'd laugh the way he laughed over and over at certain television commercials as if he were seeing them for the first time.

"You ready to be a bass?"

"Not even a baritone," I'd say with adolescent shakiness.

"Well, you're a pure and peerless tenor right now. You reach notes that the wishful tenors only dream and strain to attain." There were almost always rhyming words in Father's utterances, as if he were forever musing on drafts of an epic poem.

By the time we'd reach the church, more words would have been spoken than in any other course of our life. And on the trip home, we'd regale the refinements of anthem and benediction until the front door opened and our vocal cords shut tight. At least until Mother died. Then we'd eat and watch Mannix and Dad would drink and pass out because he had to.

Grieving Father's passing elicited deeper sadness over simpler themes. My loss was pure because his love was unfettered. This curriculum lacked the complexity of Mother's death and remains to this day, living without someone I've loved and who has loved me. Again, I felt relief, but for Father, whom God delivered from a life of regret, travail and addiction into everlasting freedom among the chorus of heaven. And as for the loss of his companionship, I found others to fill the void.

"Son," said Dr. Everson, as I scrubbed the shelves in the medicine cabinet of his private bathroom with enough cleanser to float our heads in vapor. "Have you considered life in the ministry?"

Of course, I had. The church could be my domicile until kingdom come.

But I'd never been flooded by conviction or filled by the Spirit in any palpable way. The moral force of scripture made perfect sense in light of the things I'd seen and heard, but I hadn't cried out to Jesus or even touched the hem of his garment, nor had I presented my body as a living sacrifice to the Father. The keeper of a safe religion can hardly be blamed if life has been so unsafe as to force him under the shelter of it.

But I lacked the divine unction; or as the Greek would say, the *splankna*; the guts.

"Yes," I said. "I'd like that."

"I believe," said Dr. Everson, "that we could get you a scholarship to a Christian college, and then seminary."

Flushed and swimming in pine cleaner, I almost embraced him.

"You're a fine young man, Arthur," said the pastor. "You're a worthy investment. If you need help choosing a school, let me know."

Of course, I needed the help. I needed to be re-parented. Dr. Everson accomplished some of this by proxy from his pedestal. But I needed so much more.

I looked at Whitworth and Whitman in Eastern Washington. Pacific Lutheran looked nice, but I wasn't Lutheran. I saw Multnomah and George Fox, but settled on Northwest Christian College in Eugene, Oregon. This small, earnest community welcomed me more personally and afforded the chance to attend the University of Oregon at the same time.

I graduated from high school with perfect grades, moderate honors and little notice. Always an introvert and never an athlete beyond Little League baseball, I attracted a polite circle of friends in the Chemistry Club and considered a day without the annoyance of inconsiderate jocks to be a successful one.

Dr. Everson and the choir director attended the school commencement ceremonies and the church choir held a reception for me at rehearsal. They gave me practical gifts, including a manual typewriter, from which I type this manuscript, and a thick comforter quilted by the ladies.

And I left for my first real adventure slightly upriver.

Chapter 3

It was 1964. While Northwest Christian College hardly boiled with revolutionaries, I gaped as students from the University of Oregon next door began to grow out their hair, tear off their cardigans and experiment with new paradigms in politics, racial relations, and sex. Then came the drugs.

My roommate, Chad Harbor, a freshman from Bend, Oregon, slid into each fad. Having toed every line drawn by his conservative parents, he now blew over and around every form of constraint. First, he tossed his ties in the garbage, then his razor, and ultimately ignored any purposeful regard for hygiene. I used to quip that this was one way to attain a high *rank* in our class. Which says as much about my humor as his humus. Puns are supposed to be a high form of comedy, but they enjoy only low levels of appreciation.

One day, I walked into a cloud of smoke in awful dissonance with his usual body odor.

"What is that?" I asked.

"Relax. It's only incense."

"Distinctive."

"Not as distinctive as what I burned last night."

"What do you mean?"

"Can I trust you?"

"What do you mean?"

"Not to squeal."

"What you . . . burn . . . is your business." He paused long enough to feign disinterest in my disinterest; then burst with childish exuberance.

"I tried weed."

No response from me.

"You know. Marijuana."

Still no reaction.

Then he gushed with detailed word pictures of the party at the cemetery near Mac Court, where he and other "more mature" students smoked dope, talked politics, and practiced gradations of "free sex."

Don't think I wasn't titillated by the last part. I'd heard rumors and seen snippets of raw sexuality across the street. On our Christian campus, no "public displays of affection" were tolerated by a careful code of conduct that we signed at orientation. In the raging world of secular university, "mature" students were all over each other, in between rock concerts and vomiting spells. It was early yet for war demonstrations or wanton drug abuse or flower children or the "summer of love" and the like. But all of that brewed in and around a fairly traditional life of frat houses and sorority belles. And our safe little campus, virtually across the street from the dilapidated fraternity that would once be a playground for John Belushi in *Animal House*, was an island.

"Why?" I asked Chad, only curious about the influences that lend toward acting out, and much less about the influences of the things themselves.

"What do you mean?" he said, turning my favorite question back on me.

I never explained myself and I never understood him. Chad lasted less than two years before flunking out or freaking out or both, and I never saw him again.

Between studies, choir, chapel, and innocent hall parties, life filled up. Always shy around girls, I stretched into some friendships that taught a modicum of entry-level charm. So, when Alice Stratton asked me to a Sadie Hawkins event, I knew enough to bring a corsage and hold the door and ask polite questions. Alice, by the way, carried her petite form with confidence in a way that allowed her assets fore and aft to stand out in inspirational and conspiratorial ways. I fell in love with them or with her. And though we barely touched during three years of courting, Alice teased and strutted and blushed and batted her eyes in a way that portended equal interest on her part.

"I love you, Alice," I dared to say to her on the porch of the girls' dormitory.

"That's so sweet," she said carefully. "What are your intentions?"

"I'd like to meet your parents," I said.

She arranged for a carefully chaperoned trip to Madras, where I met her quiet father and smart but stern mother. I remember little from that weekend except that I passed muster and uttered a private word of thanks that Alice was more cheerful than her mother and more forthcoming than her father, lest I should be headed toward a life too familiar to the one my parents shared. Needless to say, I hoped for a marriage that was at least collegial and at best affectionate. I had no experience in recognizing or cultivating the potential for either.

"Sir, I'd like to ask for your daughter's hand in marriage."

Mr. Stratton's eyes bulged slightly. Then he paused to edit a response laden with emotion. Finally, he said, "You have my blessing. And my prayers."

I took both in the spirit in which I wanted to hear them.

We planned a wedding in her parents' church on June 15, 1968. She, of course, poured herself into the planning in a way that made me eager for it to be over. Since I was busy with finals and graduation, it was easy to excuse Alice's disregard for me. I graduated with honors again, and even won the coveted Kendall E. Burke Award as the outstanding student. It seemed obvious by the vanilla-flavored applause that I was a safe if not popular choice. I ran in circles of older, more serious students and would have been called a nerd in the parlance of that day. Still, it was a welcome boost to my spirits during a ceremony at which I had no family other than Dr. Everson and the professors who treated me with respect and kindness.

Now, for the story of our wedding night.

It's uncomfortable to share it with you, since a son hardly wants details of his parents' sexuality. Still, my hope is that it lends understanding that leads to healing and help, even for us both. Please forgive the archaic language and stilted tone, but it suits the nature of that time and of that union.

We finished the wedding at two-thirty on a Saturday. The receptions in those days were more about receiving lines and cashews than dinner with dancing, so we were on the road to our honeymoon in Ashland by four o'clock. The ride along Interstate Five, so recently replacing slow and winding old 99, seemed to speed by. Alice recounted her highlights from the wedding. No, actually she recounted each detail that went awry and applied blame on appropriate players.

We checked into a nice old hotel a few blocks from the theaters that performed Shakespearean plays through the summer. We'd eaten a lunch that Alice's mother packed in the car. When we went to our room, a rather luxurious suite for the time, our tensions increased.

We exchanged gifts. As seemed fitting at the time, we both gave monogrammed items—a pen set for me and a journal for her—with cards that declared our love in rather formal tones.

She withdrew to the bathroom. I changed into a new pair of pajamas and rearranged the bed in a manner that seemed welcoming and not presumptuous. My only coaching had been gleaned from the school chaplain, who always showed an interest in me. He'd been frank about the mechanics but naïve about the woman I'd be marrying. But who wasn't?

After one full hour Alice opened the door, wearing a thin, floor-length robe. I suppose it was called a peignoir. Her face looked pale and her eyes nervous, so I tried to put her at ease.

When we lay together, she felt stiff and hesitant. I attempted to arouse her, but she gestured for me to move the process forward. She didn't want to be undressed fully, so I accessed the necessary parts and proceeded to have my first experience in lovemaking. As I spoke my affections tenderly, her face tightened up and her terse reply froze me. "Are you done yet?"

Oh, forgive me. No son should read such personal accounts. But it seems you must know that I discharged against a flurry of conflicted emotions and then allowed her some space. She rolled to her side, faced the window, and either slept or feigned sleep. My prayers that night, and for many nights thereafter, were sprinkled with fear.

In that way, we consummated a marriage that, I dare to confess, I soon regretted. But to salve that regret, we conceived that night a child whose life I treasure as my own.

You became, dear Donnie. My flesh and blood.

It was the only time that Alice Stratton Gilliam allowed me to love her in that way. So, you see, your life is a miracle in my eyes.

You were meant to be. I am grateful to God.

Chapter 4

"You did this to me!"

A hundred times she'd told me the same, though now hardly seemed the time. We were racing to the hospital on a wet March night in San Francisco. When we reached the hospital, Alice gave one last hateful glare from the wheelchair and disappeared into the delivery room.

Oh, she was transformed that night! Her baby boy transported her into euphoric womanhood. No post-partum depression for her. Instead, she tapped from some unknown source of affection and spilled it out on you. She adored you.

She ignored me. Even my weak attempts at participation in ordinary matters of diapers and bottles were greeted by hostile words. "That's not how you do it, you idiot!" Or, "*Give* him to me. Give him to *me*!"

I retreated. Oh, I am so sorry for how far I retreated. And dear Donnie, I fear that I'm only now returning from that desolate place to be a shadow of what I could have been for you.

But again, she loved you. She did.

Between seminary in San Anselmo and a part-time ministry position as an ill-fitted youth pastor at Village Church in Mill Valley, there were more than enough distractions. I poured myself into Greek and Hebrew, and then into bored teenagers who regarded me with some disdain unless I planned mission trips to Mexico with Disneyland tagged on. The hours are brutal for youth ministers and Alice punished me for my absence even as she despised me in my presence.

And this about you—you were a beautiful child with a temperament that brought relief to a stricken household.

Finally, dear Donnie, Mommy could not sustain her interest or affections beyond infancy. Her muscles for a life of generosity simply had not the mass or endurance. The more you became a little man, the more she applied her subtle hatred of the male gender onto you. I doubt it would have been much better if you'd been female, for she would have loved a girl in a twisted way. But, alas, you are male. As am I, or I should be.

As a protector, I failed beyond measure. Mommy had no capacity for you. I had no practice at parenting you and no spine for policing her. So, you learned to take care of yourself and I learned to respect you for it. All the while, I pretended not to notice how badly she was hurting us both. And by my cowardice I brought us all great harm.

"Your son messed up my house!" she'd say, after you'd make a toddling foray into a cupboard and clank pots and pans onto the floor.

"I'm sorry, honey."

"You know I hate it when you call me honey!"

"Yes, dear."

"Are all men so destructive? All you do is create messes."

"He's a boy," the strongest defense I could muster.

"God help us, do I know that."

"I'll take him for a few hours." I offered.

"And do what? Teach him Hebrew? Just let him be."

God forgive me, I followed her orders. To say that I placated only and always is like pronouncing that the Beatles had a few hit singles in those days. Today, therapists would call me a codependent and teach me skills for loving my wife by standing up to her and refusing to be her doormat. In those days, people only joked about domineering wives and dishrag husbands, and men went bowling and worked long hours and teased about "the old ball and chain" in the most general terms to release their animus; and finally died young of hardened arteries.

Of course, I don't bowl. And pastors aren't allowed to utter ill words about anyone, especially their wives. Therapists were unheard of, especially for pastors, and my advancement in the pastoral ranks required a combination of performance and the projection of health in my household—which no one ever probed for fear of striking hard truth.

"Aren't you going to do something about your son?" she asked, the first time you were in trouble for smoking cigarettes.

"What would you have me do?"

"Discipline him."

"Should I ground him?" I asked.

"And have him underfoot all hours? You'd be punishing me! Make him go to church with you. That's punishment enough."

So even church became an exile and not a land of promise. Your disdain for my weakness, well deserved, took form by subtle rebellions against all authority. You hardly harmed a soul, but your disregard for teachers and coaches and, well, parental figures, translated into greater isolation.

You became a loner. A bright, talented, contained and self-assured island. My feeble paddlings out to your little sanctuary were received with legitimate indifference. I remember asking permission to come into your room, praying for an opening. You'd turn up the volume on your stereo and I had no more authority to dissuade you than I had in Mommy's life.

Even that name. She insisted on being your *Mommy,* though she quit playing the part as soon as you learned to talk and walk. And I called her Mommy, since no other term of endearment fit the shapes and angles of our relationship.

I'll ask you this question many times, Donnie. If you cannot answer me, then know that I'm not blind to my shortcomings. Will you forgive me? Ever and only for yourself, so that the chain of bitterness and neglect can be broken in the family line, and so you can be free to love well.

Perhaps you've already learned. Maybe your life is marked by solid friendships and generous graces. Has God already intervened, or was God forever your quiet friend on that island retreat? I hope you have stopped guarding yourself against the pain of relational investment and have dared to expose yourself to another. If you haven't, I'd understand. But I pray 'til my last breath for you to know a trustworthy friend, and even to risk a loveworthy woman.

By the way, I loved Mommy. It was a sad love. Far less brave than *agape* and much too frustrated to be *eros,* and not reciprocated enough to be *philos,* it was the love of a beaten dog with no bite, and a ridiculous brand of deep-seeded loyalty. For better or worse, it was the only love I was able or allowed to give.

Not to help you forgive, for I am without excuse; but to help us both understand, can I indulge in some speculation on my own childhood? As my father was an alcoholic before I knew the term, so I was a dry alcoholic before the label had been invented. I escaped into studies and work rather than a bottle, but still ran hard from real issues and into a safer form of anesthetic. My codependence I learned from both parents who never confronted each other. Mother's chronic self-pity festered as completely unchallenged as Father's drinking. I never learned from them how to say the hard words, though I would have learned harsh words, if not for a rabid allergy to harshness that developed early in me.

Your childhood spooks me like a ghost haunting his old domain. You withdrew to your room and to rock music the way I had once fled to the safety of the ballpark lawns and the urine-smelly dugouts, and then to church.

To his credit, Father might have succeeded as a parent more than me. To her credit, my mother had more obvious reasons for misery than your Mommy did. In this way, your parents failed to accomplish what everyone in our generation sought—to make the world a better place for our children.

Imagine all the people.

Chapter 5

THE WORST OF IT started in San Francisco when you were three. San Francisco Theological Seminary glowered heavily over San Anselmo like a castle above an English village. Since I'd not personally experienced the transcendent God, the old buildings sufficed in a priestly way to represent the Aged One like the sanctuary of my childhood once did. Just strolling among the ghosts of so many learned theologians who'd staked their pursuit of the Divine in those hallowed halls granted to me a borrowed confidence to take my place in the grand procession.

And I felt closer to you, Donnie, than at any other time in our shared life.

You loved "the castle on the mountain." You'd pick up sticks and vanquish monsters, musketeers, marauders and any old villain that your fertile mind could conjure. I lacked the imagination or playfulness to join in. As a swordsman, I looked rather like a "pencil-necked geek," which was one of your Mommy's less hurtful descriptors—less so because it was true in the changeless way that assaulted only my exterior and not my character, which I struggled to prop up against every onslaught of her fury.

Still, you didn't need me to join in the swashbuckling. I watched and smiled as you climbed hills and walls crying, "Take that, you knave," before you knew what a knave was.

A woman in my systematic theology class had full, wavy hair and a full, wavy body. Both shook well and often, and I missed much of the body of Professor Stark's lectures wondering how it might feel to ebb and flow in the midst of my classmate's waves. Her name was Andrea.

And she noticed me.

How strange. Perhaps a lurid past pushed her toward safe, strait-laced men. Or had she tired of mindless muscle and motorcycles? Or did I invent this fantastical sense for her shared curiosity? Either way, her raging beauty figures into our story.

Mommy worked some evenings at a restaurant at the foot of the hill. I'd take you with me to the library, where you'd be utterly content with a few gadgets and books. You were an early reader and an avid one, and the quiet of the library suited you well.

On our way to the library, you were conquering assailing Vikings with a stick longer than your full height by a foot. Andrea the Tempter crossed our path. Entranced by your bright face and at least generous in her interest toward me, we broke into a long conversation about pre-, post- or amillenialism, or some other matter that theologians used to comb through in those days. Hers was a passionate post position and I listened to her views with ears almost as rapt as my eyes, which followed her voluptuous lips and slightly distended tongue as it posited itself fluidly around her teeth like a nightclub dancer smothering a pole.

After a half hour, she noticed your absence. "Where's your son?"

I chilled all over with fright, partly for you and still more for the marital consequence of any missteps involved in your care. In other words, I was terrified that Mommy would, shall we say, flip out.

Four hours later, we found you. And, yes, someone had felt it necessary to call Alice into the hunt. She poured her soul into finding you. When a cafeteria employee discovered your sleeping outline in a culvert not one hundred yards from where I'd lost sight of you, Mommy swept you into her arms and cradled you back to our apartment in student housing.

When I returned minutes later after releasing all the searchers from their efforts, she hissed at me, "You horrible man! You inept father! You stupid, pitiful fool!"

I began to explain and defend myself, but I had no grounds.

She hit me with a balled fist directly on the nose, drawing blood. Then she slapped and scratched and clawed and spit and swore at me for bloodying our carpet. She cornered me for nearly five minutes.

I didn't stop her beyond the ordinary instincts to protect my eyes and cover my privates. I'm not even sure I was much stronger than her, especially in my state of self-hatred. So, I let her pummel me until she grew tired of the exercise.

Then she pointed an index finger into my eye. "I'll never trust you with that boy again."

From that day on, she had her way with me; that is to say, the way of the tigress who has tasted blood. She knew I wouldn't leave; I was too weak to walk away and much too enamored with our son to walk out on you. She trusted me never to fight back; I was too polite. And she assumed I'd never tell a soul, or else I'd lose my reputation and standing as an upwardly mobile scholar.

She also hated herself, I now realize, and hated even more the thought of exposure, humiliation and scandal—so she'd lure me back into our affectionless marriage with partial apologies and chance glimpses of her in her underwear, as if to hint at some promise of intimacy. And then we'd fall back into cold, tense reality until the next blowup. It always came.

Years later, I understand better the affects of her early sufferings at the hands of others. And I also know the power of hormonal imbalance and menstrual cycles. If she was able to stomach my proximity for three weeks out of each month, I'll swear under oath that she wanted to tear the Adam's apple from my throat on each of the other seven days. "Hell hath no wrath like a woman scorned?" Hell hath no wrath like the woman I lived with during every period in those days that might have held so much promise.

You were relatively safe. She gave you grace, I suppose, because you weren't able to hurt her yet. You were still so soft and un-male-like and your occasional disobedience flowed out of curiosity and innocence more than insolence.

But the day you learned that trick, she turned on you. I'd seen the early signs of her bubbling rage when you'd test your boundaries like any toddler by dropping a morsel from your highchair, or when you'd stain the couch with soiled fingers. She'd recoil and then pout and slam cupboards. I hoped that Mommy's violence would never visit you and I convinced myself that her own flesh and blood would earn safe haven.

I was wrong, Donnie.

She was wrong, too, and I'll not absolve her too quickly.

Still, Donnie, a man does something. A man does anything. Your Daddy was not a man. Not yet, anyway.

Oh, Donnie.

Chapter 6

THERE IS NO PRIDE in saying that I began to flourish at church. While youth ministry fit badly, I accepted a new role at the Village Church in Eugene. It felt good to return to Eugene, a place where I'd once found a niche. Even Mommy liked that city and took pride in the standing of being the wife of a smart, favored Associate Pastor at a prestigious church. And this was *my* church, the place of my youthful curiosity. It was true sanctuary and I walked in a line of noble pastors like Dr. Everson.

Those were fine days at Village Eugene. The church's reputation as a thinker's church in a university town meant that an erudite man of words could offset his lack of zeal for the gospel with theological complexity. I'd only encountered Christ vaguely, so teaching theology and dabbling in philosophy were easier in a climate where people loved intellectual calisthenics with a dash of mysticism. As a student of many intellectual voices, my lectures informed without inspiring, since I had no honest testimony of successful lab work in the science of living faith. I found it far too easy to teach religion without experiencing deep spirituality.

Soon I adopted the social gospel like many of my peers. It seemed the path to respectability and advancement and it required little prayer or God-consciousness. Of course, the poor are always on God's heart and being an advocate for the disadvantaged puts us akin to God. But, I confess, I ran a parallel track in proximity to God without actually intersecting him.

From all evidence, my fellows in that movement covered a spectrum of thought regarding classic Christianity. I quietly embraced the ethics of collective morality because I'd suffered so many defeats in the realm of personal spirituality. For example, I wore marital crisis and every self-inflicted wound like a badge because they put me in touch with those who suffer. I gave little thought to how my failures in critical relationships and mismanagement of human covenants affected the shepherding of the local church. There is something in First Timothy about fitness for ministry, and again in Titus; but I was majoring in Old Testament prophetic literature. Not the predictive kind that pointed to the coming Savior, but to the appeal for justice. God knows I was quietly hungry for justice and empathetic toward the oppressed.

The Bible was for me a handy book of cut and paste quotes to be superimposed whenever they granted authority to my presuppositions. And those quotes didn't support my biases, or even accused them, I was quick to abase the authority of whole swaths of scripture and to apply modern criticisms that put apostolic authorship in doubt, or that placed notions of timeless truth under a cloud of suspicion. I discounted entire portions of the Bible because they were inconvenient to my cause or indicting to my character. At the time, in my own feeble way, I was on an intellectual crusade to stamp out shallow, adolescent versions of the faith. In so doing, I was commandeering God for my purposes. With God in my pocket, however small that God became, I did some good for the disenfranchised, but even more harm to the church, their greater friend.

In other words, we discounted entire portions of the Bible because they were inconvenient to our cause or indicting to our character. But at the time, we were on a crusade to stamp out shallow, intrusive evangelicalism and to commandeer God for our purposes. With God in our pockets, however small that God became, we did some good for the disenfranchised and even more harm to the church, their greatest friend.

All the while, you were a wonderful boy. Every gadget came apart in your hands as the Holy Writ came apart in mine, though you somehow fit yours together again with improvements while mine was a Humpty Dumpty religion. What you did to bikes and model airplanes, radios and finally computers astounded me then as your genius does today. Yes, Donnie, I do know where and who you are.

You were imperturbable; not involved with us, of course, for the best of reasons. Nor were you exuberant or exultant like other children. Any traces of overt revelry had been squeezed from you. But you were curious.

Once, when you were barely more that a toddler, I replaced the battery in a toy car and still couldn't get it to work. After giving up and handing you a dead car, I returned later to find you unscrewing the battery compartment and reversing the batteries. You never looked at me in triumph or disgust; you simply played with the car and logged the discovery.

Oh, I would love to see that log. Especially the feelings recorded there, so that I could understand you more and reconcile with you more completely. But even then, you locked away all of that emotion in a strong box and hid the key.

Perhaps you wish that I'd searched harder for the key? Maybe you left it in plain sight and I had no eyes to see? Donnie, I was blind, but now I see. I was lost, but now I'm found.

Will you let me know you?

The first time Mommy slapped you, I wanted to call the police. Just as I'd wanted to call a lawyer when she first hit me. But I didn't and, again, I didn't.

Few understood spousal abuse in those days, and even fewer acknowledged the abuse of wives upon husbands. While you and I found our escapes in our realms of accomplishment, we were hostages in that home.

Once, I held Mommy down to make her stop hitting me, and she bit me and spit in my face and swore that she'd call the police, the church board and the newspapers if I didn't let her up. I let her up and she hit me mercilessly until I had to spend two days in isolation and actually practiced wearing makeup for the first of many times.

More often, I left the house, dreading the likelihood that she'd visit her rage upon you; dreading even more that she'd take you away or abandon us both in her rage.

Most often, I cowered and caved and placated—damn it, did I placate.

Now I know what a better man would have done. A better man would have stood up to her from the very first day after that awful honeymoon and said, "This is unacceptable. We either get help together or this marriage is annulled." And when the violence began, a stronger husband and father would have brought in every help, exercised every kind of intervention, and answered that woman's misguided cry for mercy so that she, and we, could have been rescued from her rage.

But I lacked the courage. I watched my father master in the art of placation without confrontation. It was the only form of marriage that he knew and the only kind I learned. While my mother abused me with words and utter neglect, she implanted the subtle assumption that for a woman to be miserable and to behave abominably is the norm.

Sorry to displace blame. Forgive me, Donnie, for being what you would justifiably call a wimp. Forgive me, Mommy, for being too weak to be your knight in shining armor; too feeble to vanquish the dragon that held you captive in a dark place.

Donnie, I believe that Mommy was sexually abused, and perhaps by her own father. And her mother refused to address the problem. Grandma was a strange woman; hard and cold and afraid of scandal; a small-town socialite among people with even smaller minds. Mommy never told me why she hated men, though she told me often why she despised me. She talked around the truth by calling me ugly and stupid and smelly and skinny and an awful provider and a terrible pastor and a horrid father. What she meant to say was simply this: "Please, help me. Do something! I'm wounded and afraid and afflicted by monumental anguish. I'm dying. You help others! Why can't you help me?"

And that was the irony, Donnie. I did help others. Somehow, I could perceive and improve the state of every other living soul except your Mommy's; and yours, of course. And even my own. But I helped others.

Did I already ask you to forgive me?

Chapter 7

I CAME SO CLOSE once.

We'd actually been on a family picnic to Skinner's Butte. Such outings were uncharacteristic of our family, as you remember, simply because breaks in ritual created minefields. "Out of order" meant "out of sorts" for Mommy. We couldn't *just* grab some fast food and toys and venture to the park with spontaneous pleasure. No, she had to wear a dress with a fitted bodice and wide sweeping folds from the hip, like something she'd seen in a Monet. The victuals, painstakingly plied upon through the night, were potato salad from gourmet magazines, or marinated vegetables, or odd pâtés that no nine-year-old boy on any continent could appreciate. And the tablecloth or blanket had to be just so, weighted by baskets and umbrellas and anything both quaint and useful to withstand the onslaught of wind or errant human movement.

The breeze started it. Not really, of course. Mommy's obsession with living into a Norman Rockwell painting, coupled with a lack of sleep and a load of tension, started it. But when the wind came up, so did her fury.

First through clenched teeth.

"Dear, could you anchor the umbrella better, please?" she said. Not so bad. Actually, polite with a term of endearment thrown in.

"Not like that. Like this!" she said, and fairly wrestled the mass of spinning parts from my cautious paws and set things infuriatingly right.

"Donnie, could you clean up that mess please?" after an unfortunate drip of awful pâté. "Not like that. Use a fresh paper towel, from the basket!" Your napkin wasn't good enough, or was too good, intended for decoration not function. "Here, let me do that!" with frustration licking out like flames. "Do I have to do everything!" she did not ask but declared.

Actually, dear, you didn't have to do any of this, I thought, but never had the chutzpah to speak.

"Can I be excused?" you asked in a well-trained way. There were fields to explore and trees to climb.

"When you finish your lunch," she said.

Oh, there remained on your plate the greater part of such a ghastly feast, at least for a child, that I wanted to eat it for you. Instead, I only braced you up and cheered you on in a way intended to come alongside, but it must have seemed to you conspiratorial with Mommy.

And that's it, Donnie. She never let me conspire with you, for it placed her on the outs—the lone female failing to tame and cultivate those rude and lewd thugs. I, of course, am the farthest thing from rude. And I confess to being more lewd than she ever knew. But I was never within a country mile of being a thug. You, however, were all boy from the beginning, and though you learned quickly to contain parts of that plague, you never bought into the program—the pogrom, really.

Do you remember? You finally looked me in the eye and said, "This is so gross!"

I was terrified and proud of you at the same time.

"Do something, Daddy," she screamed. "If you don't, I will."

I took you firmly by the arm. "Finish your food, Donnie."

You flipped the plate over, face down, onto the picnic spread.

She flipped out. She began by hitting me. You started to run, but she caught your shirt and pulled you backward until you landed on top of her basket, breaking the handle.

"Let go of me," you said, without tears of outright anger.

"I will not," she said, and she began to rain blows down; open handed blows, but hard and evil.

I reached out to stop her but feared the outbreak of war. I hesitate to admit that I also scanned all around, so fearful that this public abuse might be observed and then the fishbowl life of our pastoral family shattered forever.

I did all I could do. I intercepted the twisted application of discipline by picking you up and turning you away from her, scolding you all the while, so that she'd see me working with and not against her; in which case she would have commenced to pounding us both to pulp.

Now you were crying, not from her beating, but from my abandonment to her side of the fray.

I told you to go over to a cluster of trees and to think about what you'd done. In truth, I tried to create a safe haven for you; a kind of base in a horrid form of hide and seek.

When you were safely—when you were at a distance, I turned to her. She was throwing food and dishware into the basket, cussing and harrumphing at you and me, and wailing over her martyrdom at the hands of such heathen ruffians.

I walked to her calmly. I knelt in front of her. "Why?" I asked. It might have been the strongest word I ever used on her.

It arrested her. She slowed down, picking up the last stray napkin and melting into forlorn gestures of wounded incredulity. The whole broken basket went into a garbage receptacle. Then she turned straight toward me, with hands on hips and true sadness washing over the anger.

"Because," she said.

I held my spot. This was the most intimate moment of our married lives thus far. More intimate by far than the one-time one-way foray into sexual love.

God be praised, she went on cautiously.

"Because I won't be a victim. Not ever."

Then she shrieked, with her veins popping free, "Not ever! Do you understand me? Not ever!"

I gathered courage and might even have prayed. Then I said, "I will never hurt you."

Quietly, she spit out these words, "You hurt me every day. You stare at me with those stupid, pouty looks like a helpless little weasel and you accuse me, you indict me, you torment me. You make me out to be a monster, and I'm a lady. Do you understand? I'm a lady."

This was my moment. I wanted to say, "Then you're betraying your true self." Or, "Ladies don't behave so monstrously." I could even have constructed something truly useful, like, "Let's find a way together to be a strong, healthy man and woman."

Instead, I did the thing I was most accustomed to doing; something I'd been encultured to do; something I'd been brainwashed from my earliest days to do.

I apologized.

Again.

For the nine thousandth time.

I apologized. As if I'd really been responsible for it all—the tirade, her rage, her own early suffering at the hands of others.

"I'm sorry," I said.

Not, "I'm sorry for your pain," or "I'm so sorry you've had to suffer," or "I'm so sorry that you feel so much."

I said, "I'm sorry," and in so doing, I cast a permanent curse upon our household. She needed me to help break an old and ominous spell, but instead I tossed another poison into the boiling pot of potion and let it splash and spew all over us.

She died that day. I mean, her cancer took her years later, but its seed settled into its host that day—I'm sure of it. I often thought the seed was bitterness or rage, but now know it to be despair. She rallied every ounce of emotional energy to tell me, once for all time, why she hurt so badly and inflicted hurt so lavishly. Instead of hearing her and loving her enough to walk us both onto a pathway of recovery, I did my feeble little apologetic dance.

We went down from Skinner's Butte eventually. She didn't hit you again that day.

I beat myself up for years.

Today, Donnie, I am sorry. But I'm not only sorry. I'm forgiven and resolved; changed and almost fully healed.

And I wish you well, Donnie. I mean this. I wish you to be so well. Can you and I, even through these words, find a way together to be a strong, healthy father and son?

Chapter 8

Gray skies over Eugene are like furled brows over childhood. If those brows afford just enough sternness to enforce crucial boundaries and instill appropriate fears, they'll serve to produce green buttes and fertile fields like the seed grass of the lush Willamette River Valley. But if they stay gray or heavy for too long, then the land and all who dwell therein grow a dampness of character that no intermittent rays of yellow sun can dissipate.

Mommy didn't do well with gray. It brought out the color of her aura—shadowy, rusty reds and pale greens.

Of course, it had to be such a gray day when you came home from a three-day disappearance at age fourteen. In fact, the skies had been gray from the moment we found your empty room and your satchel missing from your closet. No note. No good-bye.

When I finally came home from church that Sunday, it was so good to see you home. I'd been so worried. But your left eye already protruded in black and blue and your face and neck shone in splashes of red. The cut on your cheek still seeped blood through your makeshift bandage.

She missed church that morning, so contrary to her obsessive want to be perceived as the perfect pastor's wife. She was always front row, pulpit side, with a regal smile, dressed in smart suits and finely cut dresses that we could never quite afford. Week after week for years, she greeted congregants in formal tones of blessing and well-wishing. Posture erect and officious, she fielded affirmations of her husband's elocution and philosophical dexterity; and then berated me in the parking lot with a stream of invectives. To avoid that ritual, I'd begun scheduling appointments for the hour directly after church.

So, I didn't arrive on the home front until long after your altercation. Perhaps you have a better descriptor for all that transpired in my absence.

I was thrilled to know that you were home. Your secret departure had frightened me as it had terrified her. Yes, Mommy was scared more than angry; though like all negative emotion, her fears presented in rage. Can you believe that her anger somehow was seeded by her love, and then fertilized by fear, and even fed by the flood of relief so polluted by fury that it spilled over you in violence?

Seeing your wounds, I feared—or actually hoped—that you'd been on a binge of hard living or wanton carousing. Had you run to drugs or something worse? Three days, Donnie, you were gone. Had you been beaten by others?

Or were you beaten again by your more obvious oppressor? This was the clear answer that I tried to hope against. Am I correct in surmising that you came home to a mother literally looking down the road for her prodigal? And instead of a warm embrace, a robe on your back, slippers for your feet and rings to adorn your fingers, you met the bite of Mommy's diamond ring as it cut through your cheek?

You never said a word about her. When I asked, "Where have you been," all you did was pull out the trophy from your satchel and lay it calmly in my lap.

> *National Association of Science Education*
> *Grand Champion*
> *Don Gilliam*

Not Donnie, my name for you. Or Donald, as your Mommy called you. Don, the National Eighth Grade Champion.

How could one man feel so much in one moment? Pride laced with embarrassment; sadness for all I'd missed and elation for all you'd accomplished. The picture of where you'd been for three days filled in while the truth about your parents spilled out. You didn't want us with you in D.C. The victory wasn't ours to prize. It belonged to you, forged in your own room and poured out in your own labors in those moments and days and weeks when you conjured a pathway to turning exile into adventure and ran laughing from the host of our betrayals.

Yes, Mommy would have gloated at the contest as if she'd inspired your genius and concocted your winning project. And I would have stood like a blundering fool not knowing how to stop her, or how to stop me from being so completely useless in the face of her pretentious babblings.

For a moment, sitting on your bed, you let me look into your eyes. We connected, though I dread to think of what you saw in me. I wanted you to see love in my gaze and a fatherly phrase like, *This is my beloved son in whom I am well-pleased*. But I knew then as I know now that my eyes deceived me; as much as my paralyzed instincts for protecting my only son deceived the will of my true self and froze me in fear.

What did I see in your flaming eyes, even through your pain and fury and detachment? Joy. And I prayed a silent prayer to the God I barely knew that your joy would be full and forever.

You do understand why she hit you, don't you Donnie? Again, not to dismiss her atrocities, but she simply had no respectable language for her love; no tongue or dialect to convey all that she must have felt in her own love-starved heart. No way or means for conveying anything good or pure.

Remember when I asked you to help me install our sprinkler? Mommy wanted the finest yard in all of Eugene, so she insisted on an automated system even in a climate that dripped and drizzled all through the year. So, we cut trenches and dug out rocks and placed pipe and glued and fitted everything just so. You were marvelous. At ten years of age, you laid more than half the grid. But remember how the heads spat and fizzled at first? Impurities of every kind had infiltrated our grand design. So, we screwed off the heads and ran water through the whole works until the whole worked. As we cleared and replaced the heads, no more dirt. Functional fountain heads. Total coverage for the thirsty lawn. So much satisfaction for us. It was one of my favorite memories with you.

Donnie, your Mommy's core self got laid out in a field fraught with so many varieties of grime and dirt and slime. She was so badly infiltrated, so that I'm sure she dreaded all of her days what might come oozing out if she dared to let anyone remove those clogged dispensers, even one at a time. A culture of true malevolence crept into her soul works and clogged her arteries. Monsters evolved into being and fed on her sadness and fear and bitterness and found their voices and bared their claws.

If I'd known the gospel in those days, I'd have preached it to her. Week after week, as she sat in the front row critiquing my humble forays into cleansing truth, something would have been absorbed. One day, Jesus would have broken into her tormented mind and she would have been convinced to risk an open-heart surgery to free up her arteries again. But on those Sundays upon Sundays she heard nothing because I said nothing. One cannot teach what one does not have.

I'm not asking you to forgive her; only praying that you will, so that your own fountains will flow freely and water your soul and feed the parched world around you. You have so much to give—somehow, you were not ruined by us—but you will give more and better and joyfully if all of your innards aren't gummed up by angst toward a woman who loved you so badly from a heart so utterly congested.

By the way, I'm sorry I told her where you'd been and about the award that you'd won. Honestly, I was trying to protect you and defend you.

And I'm sorry that she broke your trophy.

Chapter 9

WHEN MY PASTOR AND mentor carried on a scandalous affair with the Children's Director, the church looked to me to step into the Senior Pastor role. Some said I had an old soul. Sometimes, tired or wounded passes for old. Many remembered me from childhood and regaled my long history at Village. And my intellect impressed the Elder Council, stacked with University of Oregon professors.

What an interesting title. I'm trying to remember what they professed. But I digress.

This was a fit made in the depths of hell. Wildly successful in previous decades, the congregation was now sprinkled with radical graduate students and their undergrad lemmings testing their wings with political ideologies that were untested by life. While the *Old Rugged Cross* crowd crowd felt increasingly marginalized, the students mobilized. While their energy helped to bring our troops home from Vietnam and too tear down hateful dividing walls, our inattention to classic elements of community life undid the church like termites in the floorboards.

First, the old giving base walked away, which included support for longstanding benevolent organizations. Those who believed in traditional evangelism gave way to people who viewed sharing the Christian message as cultural imperialism. A few of our young leaders got swept up in drugs or in the anarchy movement that was sweeping through the Old Whiteaker District near the church. And we had a pastor—me—who preached Christianity as a new brand of sociopolitical good works theology, with little regard for historic discipleship. All of this added up to the slow death of a once-great church. Too late did I learn that among all the frontiers of advocacy, on various ends of any ideological spectrum, not one or even all are an adequate replacement for Jesus Himself, who is the centerpiece of the church. Remove that one stone and the whole arch will crash down.

On my watch, that beautiful sanctuary, with domed ceiling and majestic pipes, became a cavernous tomb and a declaration of my failure. I virtually starved the church of my childhood to near-death

"You have killed this church," Mommy said. "You idiot. You take a perfectly good church, a great church, and drive it into the dirt. This is so humiliating. I can barely even look people in the eyes. I am a pariah. An absolute pariah."

She had inherited her mother's interest in social standing and at one time actually appreciated my early promotion to a prestigious pulpit. She'd even told me so during a moment of uncharacteristic kindness. Alas.

"What are we going to do now!" She pleaded with desperation in her eyes. "They're going to fire you. You know that, don't you? You're worthless. You babble on about German theologians and ancient philosophers and everybody thinks you're so smart, while the whole place is crumbling around you."

If I'd really owned my preaching, I might have justified all of this change as the viable replacement of a tired and unworthy version of church. I could have fended off critics with high-minded theology and incarnational philosophies about a new and emerging church of socially conscious people who care more for the poor and the lame than for the steeple and the pew.

But I knew better. My own soul felt as empty as the sanctuary and my small efforts at social do-gooding were running on the fumes of an empty spiritual gas tank. Was it only our church that suffered the subtle malevolence of powerless religion?

All the while, the culture around me was getting battered by waves of drug and sexual revolution. Almost every family in our church seemed to suffer at least one child suffering from addiction, and wanton sex seemed to be the new norm.

Not that I was, shall we say, *getting any.*

No. Mommy had no love to give and a bleeding sense of her own sexuality. Unfortunately, she was beautiful. She kept her figure and knew how to flirt subtly with other men, which flared my interest and then crushed it almost daily.

Unlike Father, at least in that season, I did not wander to other women. Instead, I fell into something almost as insidious. Out on the highway to Junction City, a small market sold a menacing stock of magazines. Convinced that the shopkeeper never darkened the door of a church, I slunk in and gathered a few groceries. I set them on the counter and ever-so-casually tossed a magazine upside down on the pile. The man simply tallied the bill and avoided my eyes. I knew then that he'd be a willing accomplice in a steady game of deceit.

I don't know how men avoid it today. The adult bookstore has grown legs and walked without shame into the living rooms and offices of weak humanity. I've kept myself ignorant of computers simply to keep myself at a safe distance from that utterly corrupting and generally irresistible femme fatale—the cyber mistress. I pray that you are not trapped by her wiles and do not blame you if you are. Donnie, if any of this is genetic, you began with a crippling propensity. God willing, you've overcome it, or will soon.

My supervisor, the Northwest District Bishop, was eager to fill every pulpit with modern theologians preaching a sophisticated gospel. So my job remained secure, even though the church budget shrunk to one third its previous size, attendance to once fourth, and baptisms down to none. Ironically, compassionate giving slowed to a trickle, even as my rhetoric grew. Other fellowships scooped up the disconcerted and wandering exiles as I congratulated myself for holding to a higher gospel.

More than anything Jesus himself got smaller and smaller in my hands as I reduced him from Son of God, Son of Man Savior of the World, King of the Cosmos, Miracle-Worker, Resurrected Lord, Redeemer of Humanity, Lamb of God who takes away the sins of the world…to enlightened, entirely human, misunderstood, social liberator. I shrunk Jesus down until the Christian system required no faith at all. My emaciated Jesus paled before true heroes like Martin Luther King, even though it was a robust and hearty Jesus who informed that man's prophetic courage and peaceful approach. And I referenced the Son of God on a par with Ghandi, who truly was a world changer, but was not and is not Jesus.

Now I realize how I crucified him. I'd become the new Pharisee, scourging Christ's legacy and nailing the Living Truth to a cross that for me had become as empty as my Christ-less soul. Empty songs. Empty sermons. Empty communion. The appearance of religion without the Risen Lord.

God forgive me. It was my worst sin among many others, even though I held the words that could save me and others in the palm of my hand.

The worst part was the deceit. Most of our parishioners never knew my disbelief, and subtle disdain, for the core tenets of the Christian faith. Like my affair with pornography, this theological stance meant a rhetorical dance around the critical matter of Christiantity—the matter about which the Apostle Paul said, "if this is not true, we are of all people most to be pitied."

"Do you believe in the resurrection of Christ?" I was asked more than once.

"I believe that the resurrection is one of the fundamental cornerstones of our historic Christianity."

"But do you believe that Jesus rose from the dead?"

"I believe that the testimony of Jesus' deliverance from the tomb has fueled God's church through centuries of darkness and ignorance."

"I'm asking if you believe that Jesus was dead and then alive again."

"I believe that Jesus died on the cross, suffering terrible abuse and humiliation, in solidarity with all the powerless victims of human hatred, and that the story of Christ's resurrection will forever represent the hope of the marginalized masses to find standing in a heartless world. 'Let justice roll down like. . .'"

"I'm asking if. . . oh, never mind."

And then they would walk away. I winced, I confess, at my own inability to believe and at my acquired ability to obfuscate and manipulate.

And I suffered every Christmas and Easter, as guests poured into church to celebrate God incarnate, the virgin birth and the miracle of resurrection. I wasn't mean enough to scorn the miracles , pulling all the magic out of our faith. But I *was* mean enough to seduce them into my faithless faith.

Mostly, I perplexed and disappointed. The next year, more and more of our congregation drank eggnog around the fireplace or opted for Easter egg hunts while steering clear of church, which had lost much of the sense of the immanence or transcendence of God.

Did I already say God forgive me?

Chapter 10

You remember, Donnie, our house with the bedrooms upstairs and the big front porch? You must remember the worst day of my life, and I hope the worst of yours. If you've seen still worse days, then God help you.

Mommy was on a rampage. Mondays were hard for me—adrenaline come-down, I assume. Mondays at home meant careful tiptoeing around mine fields of volatility.

Do you remember coming home from school? You went directly to your room, as was your custom. I was in the garage, at first, hiding among unnecessary chores—cleaning clean cars and ordering ordered shelves. I came in when I heard her screaming for you.

"Donald Gilliam, you come out of that room this instant!"

No response.

She marched up the stairs.

"You answer me!"

No movement behind closed doors. She burst in.

"Turn off that blasted music!"

You must have pulled off your headphones.

"Come downstairs this instant!"

"Leave me alone. . .*Mommy*."

I remember the lick of sarcasm in that word and fear jolted me to the foot of the steps.

"How dare you talk to me like that!" she yelled.

"How dare you talk to me like this," you said in a cool and calculated tone. Had you been waiting all your life to make a stand?

Then I heard the scuffling.

"Don't touch me," you said calmly.

"I'll touch you whenever I want!" she screamed.

"Get your hands off me," you warned.

But she roared like an animal.

And then she tumbled down the stairs in front of me. I saw what happened. She was pulling on you and lost her grip. You did not strike her or push her, contrary to what she told the police.

She bruised her pride more than her hipbone. After calling the police, she simply said, "I want him out of here."

It was the defining moment of the first half of my life. Thirty-eight years old; pastor of a church gasping for breath; husband of a wretched woman; father of an abused sixteen-year-old. It might have been the moment I'd been waiting for—*my* brave stand.

Oh, poor Donnie, I let her push you out of our lives. No. I pushed you. I pushed you with my cowardice, my fear, my shame. I pushed you out because you were more of a man than I was. I loved you with my heart and hated you with my actions; rather, my inaction. No greater sins of omission have been confessed in my office or on the altar in all of my ministry years.

The look on your face sears me to this day. It wasn't scorn or anger, or even hurt. You looked at me with pure disappointment, as if God had somehow granted you the ability to see me as I was—a person who meant no harm but perpetuated great harm by caving, always caving, to fears far worse than the object of them.

Mommy didn't do this to you. I did. Not to dismiss her. She must own before God the manifestations of her illness and pain and rage. But there was a stewardship in that home that belonged to me—a trust. I broke it, failed it, shredded it. I did not protect you or her from the monsters that stormed our castle. I cowered and shrank to the shadows.

When you took your GED and graduated early, I burst with joy over the man you'd become in spite of me and wept over the missed opportunity to feel fatherly pride. When you left for MIT, the vast country between us felt dark and heavy like six feet of earth separating us forever—you on the upside and me the underside. When I heard of your graduation, then your inventions and patents and finally your fortunes, I wept at the grandeur of God's redemptive designs. And I prayed that your success might salve the residue of pain that your childhood must surely have left like deep tire-tracks on an otherwise manicured lawn.

You must know that she was still more miserable after you left. She hated me with more disdain and strained for the esteem of others with more desperation, simply because she'd lost the benefits of your resident genius to prop up her standing in the world.

I don't blame you for the unanswered letters and calls. I hold myself responsible for the holidays alone with that woman or adrift in my work. How convenient to be employed in a field that rewards busyness on holidays when others are holed up together in their presents and pajamas. I suppose I began to hate her, though the membrane between love and hate is thin and porous.

It all tumbled down in three months that I barely remember. Her diagnosis left me numb with contradictions. Cervical cancer stole what little restraint she had, so that her volatile anger became a river of torment and bitterness. No one, not doctor nor nurse nor pastor nor passerby, was spared the rancor of that wasted soul.

Her death brought sweet release. I cannot lie. I celebrated in my twisted and stunted ways, with weird orgies of pornographic frenzy.

Until I realized that I was stomping on her grave, just as I'd been passive-aggressively trampling our wedding vows and ruing the day I'd married her.

On the fifth day of my revelry, I put down my magazine for the last time and cried out to God.

More of that later.

But I began to really preach. Through the pain and shame and loss and freedom, I found my voice. It wasn't good preaching, but it was heartfelt. Not informed by the fullness of the gospel, but swimming in the absoluteness of my own futility without God.

The church saw the difference. Rumors must have circulated about the pastor set free by the death of his "rather shrill" wife. A few people came back to the church.

I submitted to better authorities and pursued better advice. I became healthy enough to recognize that the church in Eugene deserved a good and strong shepherd with a lively faith. Thus did I resign in June of 1988. Forty-two years old, widowed and estranged from my only son. An embryo in an unfamiliar faith and a shepherd in a denomination that knew not the depth of my immaturity.

That is how I ended the first half of my life; more than half, actually. In my way of thinking, this was the latter end of gestation precipitating an arduous trip through the birth canal.

BOOK TWO

Introduction

ARTHUR GILLIAM'S TRANSPARENCY TEASED me right into the next bundle of papers, clipped tightly by a black and silver clasp.

"Have I met you before?" I asked Arthur, actually hoping he wouldn't answer. His resurrection would frighten me. I believed such things could happen but less that they would. And I hoped that I hadn't been his adversary during the flaming days of my youth, when I was unkind in my criticisms of pastors like Arthur.

But so went those days of the late 20th century—a new generation strapped on our ties and our orthodoxies, cut our hair and began to reclaim the church, while more than a few aging pastors were actually reborn in their own pulpits under the influence of a simpler gospel. So many of us were rescued from those frightening days, when churches with fertile histories became wastelands almost overnight, mostly because of prioritized politics, left and right, with only a little bit of Jesus thrown in the mix. The hypocrisies of both extremes were as flagrant in those days as the equal and opposites on the other side. That polarization of the church by labels and parties has proven to be the bane of the American church in the 20th Century. It's taken the *next* generation to prove how silly we were and how eager we'd all been to franchise bits and pieces of Jesus to float our biases. We don't know yet if these children of ours can rescue the church in America from obsolescence with their fresh and organic notions of community. I hope so.

"Arthur, something happened to you," I said. "Something in your narration tells me that you weren't paralyzed forever by your past or by your mealy theology. Who are you now? What did you become before you became, sorry, this?"

No visible response, except that panning of the pupils that seemed to cry out, "Read on."

So I did. I confess that I carried the manuscript out of the room to an inner courtyard, since the aroma of pee wore on me. Again, more power to those ladies who keep showing up and giving it up for Arthur and all the others.

I made a few calls on my cell phone to make sure I wasn't blowing off any appointments. My assistant seemed unmoved by any crises in the office and her tone of relative disinterest rendered some permission to stay away.

So I borrowed some coffee from the nurses' station in a Styrofoam cup—bad coffee, but strong enough to clear my head. And I kept reading. I wanted to meet the new Arthur Gilliam, or rather the next Arthur Gilliam.

Chapter 1

TAHUYA, WASHINGTON, IS A sleepy community lining the north shore of Hood Canal. Primarily a strip of waterfront vacation homes, the town proper used to be composed merely of a fire station, an age-old market, a competing mini-market and a church. Nowadays, it's less. The church serves as the centerpiece—well, the water is everything to that town—but a log-cabin-style sanctuary with attractive windows can pull one's gaze away from the water for a long moment. And then, whoosh, you're out of Tahuya proper and further along the shore of the Canal.

The word *canal* is a misnomer, of course. No one but God and glaciers could have dug it or dredged it. Deep enough to host a nuclear submarine base at Bangor, Hood Canal is actually a channel off of the Straight of Juan de Fuca. Seventy miles from mouth to toe, Hood's Channel, as I prefer to call it, digs a course shaped like a fishhook between the Olympic Peninsula and the greater part of the Evergreen State.

Tahuya sits almost on the curve of that fishhook—the less trafficked inside curve. At the smart new store, they sold "Whatsit Tahuya" tee-shirts and a wide assortment of vacationer needs. At the old Tahuya Grocery, with even older proprietors, they sold much the same fare, but with a used book-go-round where residents and visitors could stock up on paperback mysteries to fend off the blahs of dreary Northwest days and weather-impacted vacations.

I've been told that the old grocery is gone now. So, then, went half of my leadership team at the church.

They were dear octogenarians, barely supported by the income of the grocery. He, George, the head deacon and usher, in charge of the doors, lights, parking lot, and benevolent fund. She, Erma, the head deaconess, filled the communion cups and supplied the cupboards for the modest kitchen.

And George and Erma were the Search Committee that invited me to be their pastor.

Donnie, you can imagine that after the failings in Eugene, my stock ran anything but hot, and my own self-discovery as a virtual fraud led me to believe that I shouldn't shepherd a prominent flock. So, I interviewed for the Tahuya job on a bright August weekend. I fell deeply in love with the varied greens and the deep shadows of that forested waterfront. The committee of two probed deep enough to be sure that I was docile and harmless; the type who would let them run things. And they needed to know that I was ineffectual enough not to instigate revivalist stirrings, which I assure you, as I assured them, I was incapable of.

For a home, they offered a humble cabin exactly three-point-two miles up the road, just around the bend. The front of the cabin (that's waterside for you landlubbers) looked out on snowcapped Olympic peaks; most prominently a giant figure of George Washington's face in repose. The deck of the cabin crept out over a seawall and above the water at high tide and the beach at low tide.

And that I remember most—the tides. They'd swell up toward the top of the wall twice a day, and then sneak away as often to leave sixty feet of beach the length of the property. And on that beach, the tide exposed generous beds of oysters. Mussels hugged the seawall with their tough membranes. Cockles and giant clams called geoducks lay just beneath the rocks, so that a lower tide produced buckets of delicious steamers if I dug only one or two holes through the heavy rocks. Starfish dried on the beach, waiting for rescue. Jellyfish danced in the shallows. Little crabs played hide and seek under every rock of substance. Bigger crabs, Dungeness and Rock, waited offshore to be tricked into crab pots by legs of turkey or other waste meats.

And there was fishing.

As I told you before, Donnie, Father didn't, or couldn't, teach me baseball or boy things. Fishing would be first among those lapsed potentials, so I don't claim to have been a mighty fisherman at Hood's Channel. But the owners of that cabin left a few poles leaning in the corner of the kitchen, beside the refrigerator. And the freezer actually had frozen herring ready for me, as if I knew what to do with it.

That wasn't all that the owners stocked the cabin with. There were books—fine books; classic hard-bounds from the turn of the century. That's the last century, of course. *Arabian Nights, Huckleberry Finn. Dante's*

Inferno. A collection of the Grimm Brothers' dark tales. And all of them set in a wonderland for reading.

A kettle-like fireplace rose up from the middle of the floor, barely heating the house. A wall heater hardly functioned, but a few space heaters rallied to the task if I was careful not to pop circuits with too much load.

The living room was a glass house. Windows opened onto the Channel to the west and lights danced atop the water's edge at night as cars ran quietly along Highway 101 only three miles in the distance. The Olympic Mountains stretched above the forested foothills; and to the south, across five miles of water, there was an Indian reservation and game preserve, where the seals frolicked en masse. To the north, more cabins dotted the shore and one lonely mansion rose up over dilapidated piers at what once must have been a very regal waterfront estate.

And, most critical, the north windows looked out on the neighbor's cabin. It was a yellow two-story home that anyone of simple words—better words than mine—would simply call cute.

And so was she. My neighbor. Cute. Simply cute.

She is the chief character of this second story. She might have been the central figure in the whole of my story, if I'd known what to do with her.

Chapter 2

THE OWNERS ALSO LEFT binoculars. No waterfront home is complete without them. Through those lenses, the mountains draw close enough to touch. Seals, cranes, seagulls and boat after boat become subject to scrutiny and the source of endless entertainment. Since the cabin had no television, and because the expanse of windows lay always before me, I'd pause intermittently from my reading and inspect my surroundings.

On one hot September afternoon, the waters calmed to a glassy sheen. I'd been outside for much of the morning, but now came in for shade. The street-side wall had two triangular plywood sections that could be hoisted to the ceiling by strings on levers, revealing screens to let in the breeze and keep out the bugs. That day, though, there wasn't a whiff of wind and the only movement in the air was the vibration of sounds wafting from sources natural and man-made—seagulls squawking and trucks laden with logs changing gears on the highway across the Channel. It always fascinates me that sound seems to live longer and more acutely on water, and so was I determined to live that way. This simple cabin on the glorious sea had so captivated me that I felt a new man emerge.

Donnie, honestly, I didn't know she was there. She had no car in the driveway—only a boat tied to a buoy thirty yards offshore, but the boat cover made the unmoving craft look as deserted as the house.

I scanned left to right, from the great bend in the Channel, across to the power plant at Potlatch, and then to Hoodsport toward the North, before pausing to watch a seal popping up and going down and up again near the piers by Misqueti Point.

That's when movement slid into the circles of the binoculars, first as a blur while my eyes scrambled to adjust. She walked into my life from right to left, out from her sliding door and onto her deck. There was, Donnie, no subtlety to the immediate attraction I experienced, for she wore a yellow knit bikini on a tightly strung figure.

Now, my son, I've been confessional about my years under the influence of pornography. I'm susceptible, like so many others, to obsessing over the female frame. But I'd been celibate from my habits for close to a year and the passive anger that drove me into that cowardly form of adultery had dissipated with Mommy's death.

So, I'm trying to tell you, this woman and her ample though petite features landed hard upon me in a way that felt less shameful and somehow quite inspired—as if I were Adam and she were Eve in a fresh Eden.

Years before, Mommy lured me in with similar features—shapely curves and athletic legs and perfect skin. But this woman had an easy manner, comfortable in her skin and unaffected by her beauty and relative nakedness. Mommy, I must say to your certain discomfort, had as many physical assets but carried them with an air of self-consciousness and overt concern for how she walked and affected others. This woman appeared so lithe and free in that weaving of magical yarn that she might have spent all her years on a beach or on a dance floor or both.

I was enchanted. She walked to the rail and stretched, her suit straining to accomplish its purposes.

Then she looked over.

I was stunned for a moment, forgetting that this creature actually lived next door and not merely as an adornment on my lenses. When I came to reality, I did the same idiotic thing that others might have done in my stead. I dove onto the floor, humiliated and alarmed.

As I lay on that tile parquet, I tried to reason that she couldn't possibly see into my shady house from her perch in the brightest sun of the day. If I just lay here a few moments, I thought, I can preserve my dignity, crawl inconspicuously to the kitchen and pretend that I'd not been totally exposed as a voyeur.

Halfway into my strategy, that vaporous female vision became still more concrete. She banged hard on my aluminum screen door, from whence she might even have spied me groveling on the floor not twenty-five feet away.

Horrified, I stood and tiptoed to the door, where I found that she at least offered the courtesy of pretending to look away as if she hadn't seen my clumsiness.

"Hello," I said in my squeakiest voice.

"Hi!" She said in a tone that carried complex chords of emotion; bright like a flute but not light on the air; rather, heavy and mystical like a primitive instrument simple in structure but crafted by pain and storied with seasons of solitude.

Oh, Donnie, I couldn't have thought all of that in the moment, but her voice entranced me many times as I fell in love with Lisa Meyer.

She turned. "My name is Lisa. I live next door. But I guess you know that."

I swallowed hard.

"I'm so mortified that you caught me staring so."

She laughed just a bit and tried to put me at ease.

"What are you? Some kind of pervert!" she exclaimed. Then she smiled. "No biggie," she said. "We all use binoculars and telescopes around here."

"But you must think me a cad," I said, trying to own my folly and leave any absolution up to her.

Again, that little disarming laugh.

"Do I 'think you a cad?' No, I think you a man."

How refreshing.

"Do you live there?" I asked somewhat relieved by her gracious manner. "Actually, you already said that you do, if I recall."

"Indeed," she said, and I perceived that her choice of words was meant to mock my formal diction.

I reddened again.

Now she was sorry. "Just teasing," she offered, trying to retrieve my dignity. "I like the way you talk. Are you a teacher or something?"

"Of sorts," I said, not prepared at this juncture to torpedo any hope of relationship by pronouncing myself a cleric.

"Well, you can help me with my vocabulary. I dropped out of school and no one came chasing me back."

"Indeed?" I said, trying to reciprocate her teasing, and again she rewarded me with a quick laugh.

"Where's your wife?" she asked, obviously probing in a way that delighted me to no end.

"She is with God, I dare say." I tried to say it with nonchalance to spare my new acquaintance, but it was to no avail. Now was her turn to be mortified.

"I'm so. . . sorry," she managed, as her body language closed in around her front side, shoulders sagging under the weight of embarrassment and arms folded across her chest.

"You're very kind," I said. "I've had an ample season to heal and, for reasons I'll not venture into, I've even experienced some relief with her passing."

Donnie, that was the first time I'd admitted this out loud. That's the effect this Lisa Meyer had on me. She put herself so completely on deck, so to speak, that my time-honored proclivities toward reserve only melted, washed out with an ebbing tide.

"Do you like barbecued chicken?" she asked.

"Who doesn't?" I answered, and she laughed again as if I were the quirkiest sort she'd ever met.

"Indeed," she taunted with a bad British accent. "The teacher likes chicken." Then in her normal way, "But you'll have to dress down if you're coming to my house."

I looked down at my bland button-up shirt and long corduroys, and then at the awkward way that my pale skin seeped through my Birkenstock sandals. In Eugene, those shoes had been my signature, even on rainy days— a kind of membership badge declaring solidarity with the Fifth Street crowd of free-thinkers. It always seemed so much easier to put on the sandals than to actually think freely.

"All right." I said. "I'll see what I can find."

"Good," she said. "Twenty minutes. Do you need directions, or are you pretty sure you can find my house from here?"

What a tease. But not punishing me; just coaxing me out, the way my binoculars had explored the contour of her thighs and the dimples just above the rear waistband of her bottoms.

"Oh," I said, trying desperately to sound savvy, "I believe I've scoped out the path from here to there."

Not bad for a total nerd.

She flitted away without another word and I stumbled to the bedroom to find my least dorky swim trunks.

Chapter 3

I ALMOST LEVITATED OVER the rock-strewn, ankle-high weeds of my yard onto the freshly cut grass of hers. Lisa stood at the grill, still in the same garb, flipping and braising chicken.

"Greetings," I said, trying not to startle her.

"Salutations," she uttered, still goading me, and she turned to face me.

"May I help you with that?" I asked.

"I got it. It's my specialty. And you don't have the look of someone who's done a lot of grilling."

"You're perceptive," I said. "In fact, if you had handed me those tongs, I might have come undone."

"So, what does that look like—you coming undone?"

Goodness. Perceptive hardly seemed strong enough.

"You think me a tad buttoned up?" I asked.

"Oh, a *tad*," she said, mocking me and looking me up and down.

I blushed again. Would I spend every minute with this woman flushed and on the defensive? If so, then so. This was fun.

What she saw in her vertical scan was a thin, pale, studious looking man; not ugly, but with delicate qualities—thin nose, broad lips, slightly thinning sandy hair, wire-rimmed glasses, narrow shoulders under the same button-up shirt and skinny legs swimming in baggy trunks over my old Birkenstocks over white socks. Not a sexy scene.

And there she was, turned again to the grill. The strap of her top cut across a chiseled back—not hard in an uninviting way, but muscled beneath Northern European flesh—naturally fair, but now pinkish-tan from her obvious preference for scant-wear.

And her legs. This woman was a dancer, or a sprinter, or some other form of athlete such that her thighs could be so perfectly taut and her calves so defined, even in the relative repose of standing over grilling chicken.

"So," I rallied to inquire, "How do you groom your calves to such a state?" It was the bravest thing I'd ever said to a woman.

"Oh, just my calves?" she asked, and my heart almost erupted with laughter and lust. I'd never been in a conversation even remotely so transparent.

"Okay. How do you groom your figure?"

Her easy laugh and then the answer. "Roller-blading. I go to the store and back, or even into Belfair, almost every day."

"That's something in the realm of eighteen miles."

"In the realm of," she said. "And I water ski, if I can find someone to drive the boat."

I liked the implications, but trembled a bit, since I'd never done such a thing.

"It looks like a beautiful boat," I said, feeling far greater freedom to be effusive about the body that pulled her than her own.

"Thanks. It's perfect for me. Fast enough to get me around, but not freaky fast. Want to go for a ride after we eat?"

"Of course," I said, with the uncertainty of one who has rarely ventured far from shore.

We loaded our plates with saucy chicken, French bread lined in black from a brief toasting on the grill, and corn on the cob, which Lisa had wrapped in aluminum foil and roasted beside the chicken. It was all quite extraordinary, in part because of the unusual qualities of the chef and in part because I'd never eaten so casually as a guest in anyone's home—or rather in front of, since we never once went inside. The deck was ample and the breeze now softened the heat of the afternoon. Ripples formed on the Channel and goose bumps occasionally gave contour to Lisa's bare skin.

"Ready for that boat ride?" she said.

"As ready as one can be," I said.

"First time, huh?"

"First time."

"Where have you been all your life?" she asked.

"Well," I ventured, "the story has its interesting points, but the lack of water-sport would be a dry chapter."

"No pun intended."

No, actually.

She worked like a seasoned seaman, lowering the dinghy by its davit to the shallows, which lingered at mid-tide near the foot of the seawall. Then she led me down cement stairs covered with barnacles and seaweed into the knee-deep water. It was the first such excursion to the deeps for my Birkenstocks. Lisa held the pointed front end of the boat steady by leaning down in delicious ways and bracing either side. She instructed me to enter near the square rear end and find my seat. When I'd gotten comfortably uncomfortable, she climbed in like a ballet dancer, took her seat, placed the oars, and rowed us toward the buoyed boat with strength and astounding precision.

I watched with awe, especially when her stomach muscles rippled to life and rose and fell like keys on a player piano.

"How's the view," she asked, embarrassing me again for my voyeurism, now from point blank range. She seemed both flattered and a bit saddened, as if to say, "I've been places you haven't dreamed of, and as friendly as the confines of this boat are, we belong in two radically different worlds." This woman had suffered her beauty, even while she led every hand with that card.

Still seated in the dinghy, she pulled us around the larger boat so that she could unclasp a network of ties and canvas, expertly managing turns and balances and knots as if she were untying her own shoes. Then she said, "You go first."

"No, ladies first," I said, quite convinced that I needed a model to show the way out of this capsize waiting to happen and into the relative safety of the speedboat.

"Actually," she said, "If I go first, you'll get wet." She had so little confidence in my ability to balance the dinghy in her absence, and her lack thereof was warranted.

She squatted toward the middle and grasped both sides and steadied the little ship while I awkwardly stretched, climbed and fell into safe harbor. Then, as if she were an elf, she stood beside me.

"Do you swim?" she asked.

"Some," I answered.

"Life vest?" she asked.

"Oh, let's just keep it at hand," I said, choosing vanity over propriety.

I watched her straddle the huge Johnson engine and lower it from its angled tilt into full vertical and delighted in the stretching and flexing of parts that made her seem superhuman. She fairly leapt into the driver's seat, or rather onto the backrest so that she could see over the windshield instead of through it. She turned the key, the engine roared to life, and she said, "Hold on" before projecting the throttle into full forward. The nose of the boat rose up against the resistance of the water, startling me for a moment, and then settled down in the smooth sea to begin cutting a path that split behind the boat in bubbling foam like a zipper opening the face of the earth.

I realize, Donnie, that I haven't mentioned her face or hair. Obviously, the other notable parts were my early and intense interest, but her face deserves description. I said earlier that she was cute, and that's a simple but accurate adjective. Her cheeks, slightly puffed, gave a hint of roundness to her features; not like a chipmunk because her teeth weren't in any way distended, but like some other cuddly creation that we're likely to see in God's next created order. Her eyes weren't overly large but had a zeal and a dance to them that left me forever teased—almost mocked, but not from any need to see me belittled. She was truly amused by me, and by many things that she watched with keenness and sweep that caused me to feel more naked than she.

Her sandy, sun-blotched hair blew back in the salty wind with natural body and wave from its resting place between her shoulder blades and from its tuck position behind the ears. She needed no bangs in front, as she had a beautiful forehead and the kind of skin and contour that required little cover of any kind, especially under the influence of the sun. Her ears, by the way, fascinated—small and perfectly shaped, such that I noticed, which is peculiar to that woman, perhaps because the wind exposed them so well and my place in her profile invited inspection.

Then, as if we weren't going fast enough, she thrust the throttle forward still more, and now I really wondered at how fast this boat was traveling.

Chapter 4

As we plowed through the blue expanse toward the middle of the Channel, Misqueti Point faded into the terrain as little more than a promontory on an endless shoreline. Now the full length of Hood's Channel spread out to the north with a misty horizon that unfolded into the Strait of Juan de Fuca in the faraway. This gave the whole effect of leaving a broad lakefront environment and entering the true ocean as it poured and drained with quiet power to and from every carved-out piece of earth.

The other effect was pulling my eyes, however briefly, from Lisa. Without my knowing it, she'd spied my look of awe and now, over the engine's steady growl, called out, "Spectacular, isn't it?"

I looked over and nodded.

"I need some groceries," she shouted. "You okay with a stop in Hoodsport?"

I nodded again and smiled at the notion that any residents of that little berg would spy us together. Then I frowned inside at the dialogue I projected onto those observers. "What is *she* doing with *him?*"

Then I smiled again. However short-lived, this arrangement made me believe that I could possibly enjoy the company of such a woman and endure the confusion of others, however insulting.

Absolutely void of worth in mooring a boat, I watched with some embarrassment and greater amazement as Lisa sidled the boat against the dock, simultaneously positioning bumpers and shutting off the engine and manipulating two ropes until we were bound to metal gadgets with naval knots and the perfect amount of play in each rope.

Donnie, I might have learned something had my gaze been affixed wider than upon her taut hamstrings and spry shoulder blades.

She reached out a hand to me, to help me in my step across the chasm. About the moment I readied to refuse her help, a rogue wake rolled under the boat, causing me to lose my balance such that instinct reached out for aid. Her hand felt somehow petite and tough, slightly moist and very soft, and a charge traveled the length of my skinny self and left me wishing that her hand could be a permanent fixture in mine.

But she was off, and I followed, trying to stride with confidence on the faintly rocking planks. Lisa, of course, danced along as if she had some system of balances born into her constitution. I followed her into the combination bait shop, grocery store and boat repair center. She procured a bag of essentials and a bottle of Chardonnay, some crackers and sharp cheddar cheese, and gestured back toward the boat—a sixteen-foot Glastron, I later learned, with a single hull and a ninety horsepower Johnson motor.

After respecting the five miles per hour buoy, she hit the throttle again and jolted me with pleasure and fear. We left the heavy smell of oil, gas, rancid sea life, and spilled beer and rushed into the fine salt air that inspires poets and priests of finer dialect.

Lisa steered us to a vacant beach near an apparently little-used Boy Scout camp, where the rocks on the shore were finer and not so harsh on the belly of her vessel. She slid the boat onto the stones, slid her bottom onto the deep blue nose, and leaped upon the shore. Before I could fathom a manner in which to help, she'd secured the whole outfit another foot or two up the slope and tied us onto a piece of driftwood. I tried to climb out in a manner that betrayed the clumsiness of my true self.

By the time I'd labored up the rocks onto surer footing, she'd conjured the cheese, crackers and Chardonnay and already wound a corkscrew deeply into the neck, flexing her forearms and wrapping her front around the bottle in a scene from a movie about some other person's life but my own. Two plastic wine glasses appeared from no plausible place and before I'd imagined the best spot for our picnic, she'd posited herself on a very ornate piece of driftwood that appeared crafted by an artisan from the Potlatch tribe for such a moment as this.

"Come here," she said, not seductively, but undeniably. "Sit here. Let's toast."

I hadn't toasted anything with anyone in all my life. Even through all the weddings I'd officiated, they were mostly cashew and butter mint affairs, not the elaborate fetes that your generation now knows as the norm.

I sat on the driftwood next to her. She offered me my glass and said, "To new friends and beautiful places."

And it was beautiful, Donnie, to have this extraordinary new friend before me with the Olympic Peninsula billowing up in layered grandeur over her right shoulder—a lean and angular shoulder, but again, not without flesh; pinkish tan and only faintly spotted by freckles over her . . . frame.

"Do you need me to put more clothes on?" she asked, having good fun at my expense.

"Please no," I said, trying suave but managing desperation.

"So," she said, blowing a hole in the moment, "What subject do you teach?"

Thus endeth my fantasy, thought I. *She'll throw on a sweatshirt hidden in some compartment, launch the boat, fire up the engine and, if I'm lucky, drive me home to a lonely cabin.*

"I try to teach people about the Bible," I said. "I tell people about God. At the little church in Tahuya."

She looked north, away up the Channel, not moving anything but her swiveled head. Then, slightly red in the cheeks, she turned back and looked me square in the eye.

"You could have told me you were a preacher."

"It's not all I am," I retorted with what seemed severity on my part but must have sounded sad and defensive to her.

"Then you must not be a very good one."

"A good what?" I asked.

"A good preacher. I mean, isn't that sort of an all-or-nothing gig? Don't you have, like, a vow of celibacy or something?"

"Not in my denomination," I said. "Have I been too forward?"

We sat silently. She sipped her wine, looking north again.

"Lisa," I said, loving the rolling of the "L" on my teeth and the "S" as it washed across my tongue like the small waves over the rocks at my feet. "I get tired of people always distancing themselves from me when I tell them I'm a pastor. I'm sorry if I misled you in any way."

"So people judge *you* when they find out what you do. That's ironic."

"How do you mean?" I asked, trying to keep our dialogue alive.

"Aren't you the one who's supposed to be judging others? That's pretty much what you do for a living, isn't it?"

I wanted to say, "Actually no. I've never had enough moral fiber to judge another soul. I might even be improved by the conviction it takes to condemn."

Instead, I stammered, "You're talking to a jelly fish."

Now she smiled again, warming me toward her and actually warming me, since the sun now dropped into the clouds that hugged the mountaintops to the west. She seemed unmoved by the graying weather, except for some charming goose bumps.

"You're saying you're not very sure of yourself."

"Do I seem sure of myself?" I asked, earning another smile from her lovely purpling lips.

"No. You don't. In fact, it's hard for me to imagine you up in front of—what do you call it—a parish? Telling them how to live?"

Now we were talking again, and I'd weathered the first cross-examination, saved by my mealy faith and some new kind of courage to be utterly confessional.

Oh, this lady priest. Would she leave me totally exposed before her nimble transparency?

Chapter 5

BACK AT HER BUOY, she reversed her magic and ushered me to the shore. Her ministries on behalf of my inabilities touched me deeply. Then she touched me on my shoulder, stretched her tight calves until she stood on tiptoe and kissed my right cheek.

"Have I been too forward?" she asked, teasing my earlier question and probing for honesty.

"No," I said. "No." Other words or actions that others might have applied to the moment were, for me, incalculable.

"See you tomorrow?" she asked.

"Yes. Tomorrow," I said, without a thought to which day of the week the morrow happened to be, or who I might disappoint in order to see this woman again.

"Good night," she said, arms wrapped around her perfect bikini top in a self-hug that stirred me toward want of a new career as her covering and comforter.

As a token of my fortunes before this encounter, the next day was indeed Sunday. I grumbled and groaned all the way to the opening hymn. Then, beyond outright astonishment, she walked in. Lisa walked directly and confidently down the center aisle, wearing a tight, brown, short-sleeved wrap-around dress that moved with her strut like the fur on a sleek jungle cat. And yet, appeasing my fears of inappropriate amounts of disclosure, she was actually covered well, as if she knew the norms of church life. In high heels, she looked tall and slender and even elegant, but for that cute face.

Every eye in the chapel, of course, glanced over, and most held gaze or devised some means of repeated glances without the detection of spouses.

64

She looked splendid.

And a bit flushed at the cheeks, as if knowing that her entrance would be obtuse.

Stupid man that I am; I did nothing to put her at ease. I only conducted the hymn with formal gestures and uttered in my clerical tones, "Let us be seated," at the end.

The sermon, a rehash of something I'd offered up in Eugene, interested some and inspired few. It wasn't the fault of the text. "Today this scripture has come true in your hearing," said Jesus after quoting Isaiah regarding "good news to the poor" and "freedom for the captives." I made very little of Jesus' bold messianic claim, and quite a lot of Jesus' core agenda to set the oppressed on higher ground.

Afterward, all forty-seven people greeted me vigorously and half or more indicated their eagerness to attend a salmon roast in my honor that night.

When I'd shaken every hand and blessed the only child in the lot with my skinny, poor, very Caucasian "give me five," to the glee of his grandparents, I loosened my tie, walked back into the chapel, and saw her there, standing in the pulpit.

"Wow. What a trip," she said.

"How so?"

"So much power. So much authority. I could get used to this."

"Actually, it's a bit terrifying."

"How so?" she said, mimicking my formality.

"First of all, I'm not exactly a master orator," said I.

"Oh, you do all right," said she, and I nearly believed her. "You're a little stiff."

"Yes, so I've been told."

"And what's the word? Esoteric or erudite or something?"

"Perhaps."

"And with a kid in the room, you could have told at least one story."

"Quite right." Now I felt tinges of annoyance pressing out against the insides of my eyeballs.

"But it was good," she said, furling her brow and rubbing her chin.

"Should I expect you'll do me this courtesy of critiquing my efforts each week?" I asked.

"Oh, hardly. Not exactly a churchgoer, you know. Well, I used to be, as a kid."

I settled into the first pew while she continued on behind the pulpit.

"Where did you grow up?" I asked.

"Bremerton. Navy kid. We hopped around some, but mostly Bremerton. My dad was a submariner up in Bangor."

"And what church did you attend?"

"Oh, I suppose we were Catholics, though I never quite got confirmed, if you know what I mean."

"Somewhat," I said. "And how long has it been since your last visit to this church?"

"Oh, this was my first. I had to come see the talk of the town, the 'earnest young man from Oregon,' they said at Sandy's."

Sandy's, I'd already seen, was the local marina and bait shop. They called it Sandy's Resort, but that stretched any notion of *resort* like a single blanket on a double bed.

"Are you coming tonight?" I asked hopefully.

"Oh, I wouldn't miss it. You're the best preacher I've heard in ages."

"And until then?"

"I thought I'd go into Belfair for some real groceries, and then maybe go for a swim."

"Do you need company?" I asked.

"Do you need the scandal?" she asked. "It's a small town."

"I haven't acquired a reputation fit to be tarnished."

So she climbed into my tan Honda Civic, pulled her feet out of her pumps and onto my dashboard, her dress settling mid-thigh, revealing tanned and freshly shaved legs; all but for the knees. They had thin blondish hairs that seemed fitting for this Bohemian beauty.

"Eyes on the road?" she said with a note of reproof.

I felt bold, perhaps from fatigue, and uttered, "You bait and then bite."

She fell silent and stared off to the right at every passing house. I regretted immediately that I'd lost self-control. Belfair still lay ten miles away, and the car ran deathly quiet.

Miles later, she spoke.

"So, where did you grow up?"

I told her of Eugene and of my family in the vaguest terms.

"Were you happy?" she asked.

"I found happy places; happy moments."

"Ah, a survivor," she said.

"Of sorts," I said, "But others have had it worse. Were you happy?"

"As a girl. Things got complicated after that."

I waited for her to continue. She didn't.

Belfair came to us. A real grocery store appeared on the right side and I pulled into a vacant spot. We shopped separately, as it turned out, since I'd not stocked the shelves of my new little home and having a woman with me raised my attentiveness to the kinds of things required for survival—and now, even, for occasional hospitality.

When we met at the car, we loaded it up and down with groceries and then added ourselves to the burden of my little Honda. It handled heavily on the serpentine North Shore Road but did its duty; all I ever asked of a car. I stopped at the church.

"Your car?" I asked.

"Oh, I parked the boat at Sandy's."

"That's a mile north. You walked in those heels?"

"I'm resourceful."

I imagined her hitching a ride easily with a delighted fisherman or walking barefoot along the edge of the road. She did not explain herself and I chose not to pry.

I drove her to the resort and offered to help her haul groceries from car to boat. "I live next door," she said. I blushed as I watched her untie and roar away from the dock yelling, "Race ya!"

The last image I saw was of Lisa sitting on top of the backrest of the driver's seat, wind blowing her dress and hair wildly, and her white-rimmed wake cutting deeply into the blue sea and rolling outward in angular courses toward either shore.

I climbed back into the Honda, backed out of the resort, sped up the highway, and scanned the waters to my left until I spotted Lisa and her boat bouncing over choppy waters toward our neighboring cabins.

The car, of course, traveled faster by a few knots, even with some twists and turns. This left me wrestling the dilemma of whether to win or lose this race. Finally, she struck me as a woman who would enjoy the upper hand, so I made sure not to pull into the weeds beside my cabin until I saw her boat zip past. Then I climbed out.

"Slow poke!" she called out, as she tied onto the buoy.

I thought I was doing well just to keep up.

Chapter 6

THERE WERE, OF COURSE, church responsibilities. Every few weeks, a parishioner would suffer a medical crisis that invited a show of concern on the part of the pastor. With no secretary, I printed Sunday bulletins and published a monthly rag overstuffed with newsy notices and sappy quotations. And the Council met bi-monthly to debate the dramas of leaky faucets and cracks in the sidewalk.

But as a whole, this was a brand of church that wanted to be left alone, save for the hope of stimulating sermons, familiar liturgies and traditional hymns. No evangelism effort. No mission program beyond prescribed checks to the denomination.

As for the sermons, these folks were as susceptible to change as a moss-covered wall. This worked well, since I'd proven myself incapable of stirring real transformation, especially since I'd abandoned any fervent leftist rhetoric for an utterly vanilla feel-good form of philosophical Christian pandering.

The only lively participant in the entire congregation proved to be the inquirer from the cabin next door, who increased attendance by more than just one simply by plopping her considerable mystique into the second row week after week. Her choice of wardrobe alone, always tasteful but chic and well-fitted to distraction, must have grown that body of believers by eleven or twelve souls in a matter of weeks. She was our best evangelism program.

And she didn't just listen.

"Why do you read the Bible from the lectern-thingy on the left and preach your sermon from the pulpit-doohickey on the right?"

"Tradition I suppose."

"It seems to me that you do it so that you don't have to tie in what you read from the lectern with what you say from the pulpit."

I thought a few moments and then offered my best defense. Silence.

"You do believe in the Bible, don't you?" she asked.

"Of course," I said without conviction. "It's been guiding God's church for a long time and some of the greatest words ever spoken come straight from that book."

We were sitting in the pews after the crowd had dissipated—actually, she lay on her back along a pew, staring at the rafters, looking either like a beautiful corpse lying in state or a lovely child making sense of the clouds.

"Okay, so you believe this God of the Bible is the real deal?"

"In a manner of speaking."

"What the heck does that mean? 'In a manner of speaking, in other words, all things being equal, as it were,'" she said in a remarkable imitation of William F. Buckley, especially coming from a woman's voice box.

I thought and then volleyed, "For some people, life's a bumper sticker. 'God said it. I believe it. That settles it.' To me, there are nuances. What, or which, did God really say? God said it through human agents. We interpret it through human lenses. We believe it through human filters. And nothing this side of heaven is ever quite settled."

Her marvelous mind churned. Then she said, "Okay, take your scripture today. Colossians something? It says that Jesus is the image of the invisible God."

"You were listening," I said, sounding so patronizing that she would have been within her rights to rise from her pew and smack me. I'd been smacked for less.

"I was listening and reading. I assume that the Bibles are put in these little cubbies for a reason—though the book I had was so stiff I'm not sure anyone ever uses it.

"So," she insisted, "do you believe that Jesus is the tangible, visible form of the invisible God?"

"That's what orthodox Christianity teaches."

"What's this orthodox thing? Are you saying that there are Christians who believe in Christianity and Christians who don't?"

"No," I said quickly. "I'm only suggesting a continuum."

"So where are you on the continuum in this case—the part about Jesus being 'God in a bod'? Arthur, it says it like five different ways in that one section. It says that God was pleased to have his fullness dwell in Jesus."

I shuddered at how swiftly her mind worked and wondered if I could retreat quickly to boat and bikini. *That* Lisa was hard enough to handle, but *this* Lisa could not be managed in the least.

"Arthur," she continued, "that's a lot of gall to say that about Jesus, and I understand if you don't have the courage to, especially in today's world; but if it's true, and someone really does believe it, well, doesn't it just change everything?"

"Indeed," I said.

She was willing to accept my flimsy response as mental ascent and personal profession; though, Donnie, I confess to far less. Up to that point I knew theology but knew not Jesus.

"And that part about being alienated from God. That's so me. I've been mad at God and I assume God's mad at me. I'll go into that later. But this says that the whole 'God in a bod' thing reconciles me and God; though I don't see how his death pulls that off. But Arthur, if this stuff is true, how can you be so stinking boring about the whole thing?"

I almost fainted.

"Sorry," she said. "No, actually I'm not. Arthur, if you don't believe all this, I understand your reticence about pretending too much that you do, though I can't really understand pretending enough to be a pastor in the first place. But if you do believe this, then this whole mess is bigger than the pet rock!" In those days, Donnie, people sold rocks and, well, you must remember. Did we ever buy you a pet rock?

I digress. Donnie, she nailed me to the door like Luther and his ninety-five theses. She was relentless, and even more so when she got to Galatians and Ephesians and Philippians. After that, she read all four gospels in one night and informed me that she wept with Martha, Mary and Jesus at the death of Lazarus and that she was "totally bummed out by the Pharisees."

Finally, somewhere around the middle of Romans, Lisa invented her own version of the sinner's prayer. She wrote her personalized creed; prodigious to the point of frightening. At last, she penned a personal mission statement based on the Great Commission, the Great Commandment, the Golden Rule and the words from Jesus to the woman caught in adultery. I can't quote it, mind you, but its essence rings and stings and echoes through my being.

For while I wallowed in impotent religion, my Lisa, to borrow her term, "got the Spirit" and became a full-fledged, Bible-quoting, ever-praying, absolutely enflamed Christian woman.

I say "my Lisa" because I was, by now, awfully smitten. What her body began, her passion brought to fullness and flower, until I loved her like I'd never loved another.

Though I loved her much, I confess that I did not love her *well*. I cringe to tell you, Donnie, that at some point on her journey between her first day in church and her first moment in Christ, we had begun to share a bed.

Chapter 7

"WHAT DO YOU SEE in me?" I asked one night as we sat on split logs, browning marshmallows in a summer ritual that Lisa swore would alter me forever.

"Innocence. Safety. I can handle you," she added, with an impish grin that the firelight amplified into pure witchery.

"What if I don't want to be safe?" I asked, and she laughed out loud as if a rabbit were ruminating about the benefits of an ear augmentation.

"Seriously," I said, trying not to sound hurt. "I've always been such a coward. Not enough moral courage to be very good at anything and not nearly enough immoral courage to be bad. So where does that leave me?"

"Well," she said in honest consolation, "for starters, it leaves you eating s'mores with a hot woman in a string bikini."

And she was right. She wore only a partially zipped sweatshirt over one of my favorite two-piece outfits, as if she were impervious to the onset of a cool night.

"How true," I added. "But it feels temporary; ultimately too much for me, as if you'll fly away soon and rejoin your kind and I'll crawl back into my hole and grow still more adept at being invisible."

"Oh, use the word *adept* in another sentence. That one always gets my heart all a-flutter!"

"See? I'm from another world, and I can't find a place or a person to belong to."

This was the most transparent truth I'd uttered to that day.

"You belong to me," she said. "I own you," and again, her jesting leaped out of her eyes and into the fire like a spark traveling against all reason.

"So, I'm your sex slave," I said, fearing right away that I'd crossed the line into some perilous part of her story.

Lisa roared with laughter until she fell onto the pebbles and rolled to the top of the seawall. Then, to one-up me, she toppled into the frigid water, which had quietly crept up the wall until it lay only three feet from the top of its rampart. As I jumped up to track her movements, I saw only her sweatshirt splayed on the surface.

To alarm me further, she swam underwater for more than thirty seconds and popped up like a seal twenty-five yards from shore.

"Come on," she called.

This would be a first for me. Night swimming terrified me and this was, after all, ocean. Shark sightings were rare excepting the little sand sharks that stole our bait every time we fished. But this moment looked too much like the opening scene of *Jaws*.

"Jump, you fool!" she coaxed.

So I did. I jumped. Not gracefully, and with so little lift that my feet hit the pebbles at the foot of the wall and sent a jolt through my being that left my ears ringing. But the water felt strangely warm after the initial insult so that I recovered and swam, following her splashing, out to the buoy, onto the boat, and into her arms.

"See? You can be dangerous," she said, after catching her breath.

"Who's the dangerous one?" I panted.

"What? Do I scare you?"

"Completely."

"Am I too much for you?"

"Always."

"Do you want me to change?"

"Never."

And that was my sin, Donnie. Lisa's wounds, which she so craftily hid behind her nakedness, needed healing; not the ministrations of a sophomoric lover. Yes, I loved her the way I gawked over my second-grade teacher with her shapely legs and undying enthusiasm for bettering me. And I might even have afforded some balm for Lisa's wounds; at least enough to stave off the infectious aftereffects of abuse. And, like with your mother, what abuse I can only imagine.

But I did her no good. And I confess that I *meant* her no good. Does the barnacle cling to the shell of an oyster with even one tentacle of altruism? No, the barnacle is a survivor, and so was I sustained by clinging to Lisa's glorious shell, which certainly held a pearl in its smooth and succulent deeper parts, but without her self-knowledge or the courage to be shucked. I explored obvious pathways with curiosity and growing extravagance, but it was a well-worn path that led primarily to the epicenter of the wound, where I might only have exacerbated the hurt.

A finer man than me, under the influence of the master healer, could have shucked her and filtered out the goo and shrapnel to seize the pearl and cherish it—her—until death's translation. Like a treasure hidden in a field.

But I was worse than a novice lover. I was an imbecile; clumsy and desperate and self-involved, like a frisky dog glommed onto an object kind enough to hold still for an exhibition of my worst instincts. Yet others had stained her so much worse that I seemed harmless to her; simple and manageable.

Too hard on myself, you might ask? No, I'm only describing a truth for which God has rendered more than adequate cleansing and for which I am learning the regenerative helps of searing objectivity. With the guiding influence of hope, I can even see myself to absolution—playing the priest and waving grace over my sorry old self until I am the object of my own burgeoning capacity for charity. As Lewis writes in an essay on "The Ego and Self," one day this old fool "may then be able to love himself as his neighbor: that is, with charity instead of partiality."

I loved Lisa an awful lot, and awfully. She loved me better but less. And we swam and played and kissed and talked and fondled like teenagers in our own *Blue Lagoon*.

And then one of us grew up.

Chapter 8

THE SEX STARTED WITH the flirting. She exhibited so much aplomb. I, for a change, found a freedom with Lisa unlike any I'd known. Then came the touching.

We were on a floating square of dock, in front of the cabin beyond hers. It was late September and most of the summer crowd had closed up their homes after Labor Day. But it was hot, like the dog days of September can get, even in Washington.

She in her bikini. I in my dungarees. She wanted lotion, though I knew that her tan had been established months before and that she was inviting me to rub her back. I trembled as I did so, rubbing her delectable skin with lotion until the latter began to peel off in tiny, dark clumps.

Donnie, it was the finest thrill of my life to that point, your birth excepted, and though I'm ashamed of what came after, I'm not lying to tell you that my bankrupt life found currency in her affection and my heart a sense of worth—to be wanted by such a woman. Why, Donnie, I came alive.

But it was only my first life finding its second wind; quite a wind, I should add. Gale force.

We did not leave that dock until it scraped its foam pontoons onto the oysters and barnacled rocks of low tide.

Still, Donnie, here is the sad part.

For weeks, we went back and forth between cabins; more nights together. More of each day in each other's company. Beyond all imagining, she began to love me. Not just sexually, but with questions and affirmations plus a hunger to be in my company that healed a lifetime of insecurity.

She told me her story. Stories, tragedies really, of robust and ribald men who abused her, abandoned her and left her doubting the male gender as much as her own ability to choose among them. Eventually, she chose instead a cabin on the water with the money from an extremely handsome settlement.

And then came this harmless preacher from the log cabin church in Tahuya. Safe. Gentle to the point of effeminate. A good listener. A curious lover with childlike innocence and barely a hair on his chest.

Oh, Donnie. I loved her so. And we cleansed each other and filled each other with waves and tides of pleasure without care.

At one level, I knew this was deathly wrong. Our intimacy should have waited for a better day when vows and proper spiritual moorings could have bound us in better order. But our sadness couldn't wait on ceremony and our bodies wound our stories into one until we wed in that crass and common way that weaves the stuff of tragedies.

So when Lisa received the love of Jesus and became a knowing child of God and fellow heir with Christ, we were also sexually active—addicted, you might say.

And then she learned too much.

"What does this part about 'yoked together with unbelievers' mean?" she asked while reading from *I Corinthians*.

"Some say it's talking about marriage. Others apply it to business."

"So why would the Bible teach us not to be yoked to unbelievers?"

I began to sweat. "I suppose so that we aren't bound to people who don't share our core values; so that we don't find ourselves compromising on our covenants with God for the sake of lesser covenants."

"Like us," she replied.

"Explain, please."

"Like us. Like our relationship. Everything I'm reading tells me that our sexual life together is premature. I didn't know that, Arthur. All I've ever known in my life is sex first, disappointment later."

I wanted to say that I didn't know better, either. I longed to tell Lisa that I'd known sex only once, and loveless sex at that. I wanted her to know how she rescued me as a man, how she poured value into my life with every stroke and sensation.

But I *did* know better, and she knew I knew.

"You took advantage of me, Arthur."

"No. No, Lisa. I loved you. I love you now. Yes, I'm weak, but the love is real."

"But the faith, Arthur; is that real? If it were, wouldn't you put my soul ahead of my body?"

"Lisa, it's not that simple."

"Right, do you have a bumper sticker for that one? 'Christians aren't perfect. Just forgiven.' How convenient."

She started to rage. I froze. Oh, Donnie. It felt familiar and so went my response. I cowed and clammed up tight like the butter clams we'd dug up and shucked that very morning for lunch.

It was pitiful. I was pitiful. A bigger man would have held her, or probed for every last emotion, pushing back at the falsehood and pulling out the truth until frailty and faith could have found peace together.

But Donnie, I didn't know Jesus. His ways, however familiar in principle, were not part of me.

Her anger subsided. In a matter of days, she even forgave me. But as she grew in Christ, day by day, Lisa saw me for who I really was—a weak man with not an iota of the faith necessary to be yoked into her virile and voracious appetite for Jesus. I tell you with no animus, she outgrew me as a spiritual being in a matter of moments at receiving Christ; she outshone me as a human being even before that. Her curious faith and clear propensity for discipleship left me leagues behind her within weeks.

As her anger subsided, so did her interest in me. She'd known all along that I was less than an agent in her conversion. She rightly gave God the credit for putting me in her life long enough to coax her to church (a feeble church though it was) and into the Scriptures (where I offered little real help).

She wasn't hurtful, but I was grievously wounded. She only showed me kindness but withdrew all physical intimacy. When she'd read more, prayed more, and forgiven more, she began to hug me, tease me, and treat me as a brother, even knowing that my faith was not hers—rather, hers was not actually mine.

In one sense, I lost her respect, since she could not tolerate a preacher who spoke out of emptiness like a white-washed tomb. In another sense, she respected me more, as a broken human being with tragic flaws. In total truth, she saw me the way I should have seen her from the start—as a wayward prodigal in need of God's embrace—but I had no reference point for that view. And now, so quickly, she did.

In short, she pitied me. This did an opposite work from what her affections had administered, so that now I felt quite low. Desperate, even.

Then on January 19th, she came to tell me that she was leaving. She'd found a job and a church and a home in Seattle. She absolutely radiated with grace, and her flirtatious manner had given way to an assurance that slew me.

"Will I see you again?" I asked.

"I think it's best . . . " she stopped short.

"I don't understand. It's best not to?"

"It's best to just hold that possibility in trust. When the time is right."

"You mean you'll give us another chance?"

"No, Arthur. I mean that your child will want to meet you someday."

Chapter 9

So, Donnie, you have a sibling. A sister, to be more forthcoming.

You might justifiably say, "Forthcoming? Hardly!"

But by my silence I've only honored the wishes of a woman wronged—a noble person who has every right to apportion information in the interest of her daughter.

Whose name, I've been told, is Gretchen. She's a teen as I write this tale, but she might be any age by the time the story reaches you. Please, if you receive this startling disclosure, handle it with care—not that I question your discretion. It's only that my offspring deserve the best, in light of what I have put each of you through.

I believe it best to inform you that you are anything but alone. God is with you, of course, but so is a young lady who shares the singularity of your father's genetic line. Perhaps in this life you will get to know and love her. I am trusting that the next life will afford me that monumental gain, however unmerited.

As resourceful as you are, she can be found. Your discernment will guide you in that way. I wish for you both the blessing of companionship, and even greater understanding of the perplexities of your origins, for having compared notes and stories.

As for me, the knowledge of this child in the womb undid me; though the separation from Lisa had accomplished much of that work already. I almost ceased functioning. Fortunately, the church required so little that I was undeterred in merely regurgitating tired homilies from Eugene and affording the most impersonal kind of service at funerals and weddings. For two sorry years I went on, hardly wearing a watch, but living rather by the rhythms of the tide that lay bare the beach twice each day and left organisms drying out, barely breathing and often hiding until the next conspiracy of moon and molecules could rescue some.

That cabin will forever be both tomb and cocoon for me. By all appearances this side of heaven, I was a dying organism. As surely as an oyster pushed by the waves of an extraordinary tide to a resting place beyond any regular high-water mark, I lay parched and desperate in my shell, too ashamed even to hope for relief.

It did come, of course. First, relief came by way of nature itself. My shell had windows. The changing surface of the water from gray to blue and back again—and often colored by splendid sunsets directly before me—gave me breath. The movements from glassy calm to white-capped chaos and back again proved to me that no storm, and not even the doldrums, can withstand other pressures and powers.

I watched the seagulls make peace—no, they made joy—with the worst of weathers. They laughed against the wind and screamed with pleasure riding it.

The Olympic peaks, and President Washington's immovable repose, held their poise through gales and blizzards and steady drizzle, and changed only their coats from white to speckled in changing seasons.

Even the crustaceans cried out with a gospel of determined will—to live and eat and reproduce in the face of predators and an ecosystem so cold and calculated that better souls might go crabby with cynicism about any notion of a benevolent, involved creator.

Finally, the seals saved me. Several times a day, they popped up as if to check on my well-being on orders from above—furry angels with floppy fins where their wings ought to have been. They made me smile. Though I couldn't recognize one from another with only their black shiny heads and ample bottoms emerging, they became my only true friends. In my imaginings, they were the best of neighbors checking in on one of their own after injury or surgery. Especially in winter months, when the vacationers had all gone home, I had the seals to myself, and they had my soul to tend after. I loved them.

Then, one memorable day, two killer whales finished their unusual inland trek by leaping and dancing and kawhooshing directly in front of my cabin—fifty miles from their normal courses—and then turned north again. It all felt as though God choreographed their visitation, urging them to splash into my curious estate, before releasing them to get on with their annual rites and passages in other waterways. I've never heard of any other sighting so far south and can only assume divine influence—though only recently have I allowed myself such speculation, since until now I wouldn't have considered myself worth pursuing with such strenuous efforts.

Oh, Donnie, God began saving me in those days. I'd learned in seminary about how God reveals himself—naturally through the beauty and symmetry of creation; specially through the Word and the prophets; and personally, through Jesus, God's Son. But it all felt like fodder for the next exam, or like the speculations of abstract theologians trying to lend credibility to their underappreciated science.

God met me there, at Hood's Channel, and I met God. Oh, I wasn't Christian yet. I became a God-lover because I loved the artist who painted the tableau before me, framed by the windows of that humble cabin.

Seeing what I now saw, I wondered that I'd been blind up to that point. Eugene was a lovely place to grow up; but pain might have kept me from seeing the connection between craft and craftsman. Two lovely women, the most exquisite of God's handiwork, should have pointed to God as surely as evergreens point to the heavens; but the first of my lovelies had been marred by tragedies beyond my knowing, and the second tarnished by me. Shame blinded me, and sometimes, somehow, Lisa did. Her form filled the whole frame of my capacity to hallow God by evidence of his workmanship.

When I came into the light of God's goodness, I saw myself for who I am—another of his works yet broken and too much the spiritual infant to be a pastor. Like a pup just opening his eyes, I wasn't the one to lead others in the frolic of faith.

The Tahuya Church received my resignation without much interest. I began asking God to show me a real calling.

BOOK THREE

Introduction

SOMETHING ABOUT THE TONE of Arthur's written voice told me that this story—the third one—must have a happy ending. How else could he have disclosed such profound seasons of failure with so much honesty and perspective?

But as curious as I was, the stench of urine screamed "stay away" and the courtyard was uncomfortable. I informed the front desk that I was borrowing Mr. Gilliam's personal memoirs. The woman behind the counter looked into my eyes for a moment and gave me a trusting look.

"It's the saddest story," I told my wife Sherri as we sat on the balcony, overlooking the Del Mar Racetrack across the street and the Pacific Ocean beyond it.

"Who is this guy?" she asked.

"A pastor, I guess, though so far in the story he's a flake. I mean, he's half victim, half idiot, but I get the sense that he turns out all right."

"How do you know?"

"He hasn't killed himself."

"Literally?"

"I don't know. One way or another. If my life were as vapid as his, I'd seriously drink myself to death, or buy a fast car and see what it could do on the Pacific Coast Highway."

"Vapid? That's quite a word for you," Sherri teased.

"I know. Reading this guy makes me feel like I have a vocabulary of twelve words; so maybe I'm compensating."

"Is he a good writer?" she asked.

"If you like Alex Trebek humor."

"Why the interest then?"

"He's pitiable, I guess. There I go again. Plus, his life is in my hands, I suppose."

"Pretty melodramatic."

"I know. But it feels like a kind of trust—his testimony; maybe even his family. Like God has a role for me to play in finishing this guy's story. Like I'm a guardian of his legacy."

Sherri quit teasing and probing and accepted that I was both serious and moved by this Arthur Gilliam's existence.

"Anything I can do?" she asked.

"Would it be rude if I finished his story tonight?"

"Not if you rub my feet," Sherri said.

She pronated her painted toenails across the space between us and rested her heels on my lap. I began to dig my fingers into the sides of her left heel, and then into the ball of her foot. By the time I reached her toes, I was into the story again. Absentmindedly, I tugged and twisted her appendages with too much torque, and I hardly noticed when she slid her feet away and slipped through the French doors and into her own hobbies.

"Well, Arthur, let's see if things get better. I believe in you, buddy. At least I want to."

Chapter 1

THE ONLY DOORS THAT flung open led to Rwanda. A position at a mission school in the mountains northeast of Kigali seemed my only pathway to becoming. American churches didn't or wouldn't touch me, after two somewhat disastrous pastorates. Any ardent interviewer would have extracted the state of my vital relationships—most notably the oblique nature of my Christology. It seemed safest and best to submit myself to people for whom English was a third or fourth language on a continent still dark enough to afford some shadows in which to linger quietly until I found myself and my faith, or else they found me. At the very least, it meant a fresh beginning in a context where my love for God's artistry found a new set of images on display.

And they were on display, Donnie. Have you been to Rwanda?

Kigali is a city set on hills—steep hills, like something I'd expect to see in Chile. Unlike American cities, where the poor frequent the valley and rich pose on hillsides, the Rwandan rich live near the sources of water and commerce, while the poor straddle the hills and squat in every unexpected crevice. But the overall effect, with the exception of human squalor, is a wonderland of color and smell and sensation.

I've never been to the Caribbean, but if I had, I imagine that the lush vegetation would remind me of Rwanda, where banana trees and every kind of fruit and produce grow wherever people have the ingenuity to cut terraces into steep hillsides. Because the place is snug and nigh to the equator, even the high elevations over ten thousand feet are mild and the climate perfectly pleasant.

Oh, the peoples, Donnie, they are phenomenal. The men are lean and strong and ingenious. The women are—oh, God help me with this— simply stupendous. Tall with shades of chocolate skin; proud bearing, especially with huge loads of produce, or giant tubs of water, or even fags of firewood riding on their heads. Their tail ends operate in the most inspiring way— not wide from the rear view, for they are all well exercised by the demands of daily life—but wide from the side. I'm trying to say, Donnie, that their stomachs are hard and flat, but their posteriors protrude, creating the most alarming notion that they could out-run a cheetah or out-climb a ram. Most, it seemed, were as tall or taller than me, and the way they smiled into the face of hardship lent them a quality of superhuman dignity. All in all, they had the strength of wildebeests and the beauty of gazelles.

The men, who I described favorably in brief, seemed quite overmatched by their partners, who looked more engaged with life and industrious. In fact, it looked as if this culture, like others I've studied, allowed some men to chew the fat and stoke their importance in debate and debacle of every kind, while the women quietly made the world go around.

No culture displayed that tendency like the Maasai, in Kenya, whom I had opportunity to observe during one of my leaves. No people could be more colorful than the Maasai in their red garb, for they are truly the post-card fodder of the continent. But only hours among them reveal that men have fashioned a well-served life for themselves, where women and children do all the work and men play war games until the age of twenty-five, when they are free to marry girls as young as nine, who are circumcised—muti-lated, really—for a pleasureless life among lazy and all-too-well-protected males old enough to be their fathers.

The Rwandan women would tolerate no such thing, it seemed, and yet the crops still needed transporting and the children cried out for a nurtur-ing presence. This left women, as in much the earth over, doing more than the lion's share.

I fell in love with many of those women, though love's form was less infatuation or lust and more respect than in my previous accounts, and no Rwandan woman ever returned the measure of favor I held toward them, which I could no more hide than the paleness of my skin.

The only ugliness was in the air. Both the nauseating pollution of unregulated auto exhaust and the unchecked ethnic tension. As for pollu-tion, Kigali roiled in gloom, and whenever traffic backed up, the ingestion of toxic fumes turned insufferable. Once out of Kigali, the overall effect lessened. But travel itself was suffocating under the influence of trucks and spewing cars clawing their way uphill toward our destination, three gasping and gagging hours from the city.

But the greater sickness at play was racism. I was surprised that, in a matter of days, I could usually distinguish between Hutu and Tutsi with some accuracy, though to make that distinction was to play into a most awful instinct that would bear worse consequences. Before landing in Africa, I'd not really been aware of regional differences in skin color, facial structure, size, and shape among all the peoples of that huge continent—but they exist, and they contribute to the tribal strains and stresses that seem remote to Caucasian Westerners who splay ignorance and nonsense about how "they are all the same." Of course, *they* aren't as we aren't.

And this became obvious quickly. The Hutu people were generally shorter, darker and had a long history of being treated as a second class, especially by colonial powers in centuries past.

The Tutsi population often stood taller and appeared fairer, and their favored treatment by colonial overlords, especially the Dutch, painted their fate as a resented subculture.

If perception had basis in reality, the Tutsis were better represented among the wealthier, more educated and influential classes. Perhaps the Tutsis more quickly adopted western ways under the influence of foreign occupation. Or in days past, they might have organized under industrious leaders or possessed the more fruitful lands. All in all, they seemed to be empowered with more freedom, influence and resources.

The Hutus certainly felt a corresponding poverty in both life necessities and civilized advancements. Rwandan history is scarred by uprisings of the common people—mostly Hutus—accompanied by bloodshed and abuse of every kind, all in pursuit of their fair share.

But this was an ugly time. Hutu teens and children rallied and marched in calculated blitzkriegs of propaganda, as if they'd been mentored by none other than Himmler. The smallest skirmishes carried insidious potential for war, such that even supposed friends who shared neighborhoods and job environments with the other ethnicities interacted in guarded ways, as if it might be emotionally dangerous to become attached to someone you might be asked to kill in days to come.

Our school was no exception.

Leaving the Kenyan Air 727, I walked onto the tarmac, immediately struck by the lush surroundings and the friendly temperatures even in November. It was spring there, as you realize. The airport itself was metropolitan enough, though the guards and officers who checked luggage and passports showed no good humor for the task, and their guns—some kind of repeat action artillery that I could never hope to name—made me feel unsafe even if they were intended to protect. If such weapons exist in

American checkpoints, they are pointed from hidden ramparts at unwary citizenry. I prefer not seeing or knowing, I think.

The school sent a car—a kind of all-terrain vehicle that spewed so much waste that in America I would have carried an apology sign in my back window. While I adored riding speechlessly through Kigali, watching clamoring humanity and imbibing the whole scene of noble chaos, my skin color and implied status made me uncomfortable. First, I felt watched. Worse, I felt the bile of pride ebbing—that sick superiority that we Americans carry with us into foreign lands. We're usually immune to our own buffoonery and insensible even to our subtle self-loathing. But I was no novice at self-loathing and tasted its familiar reprisal in my throat. I sensed already that my ethnicity would afford me some immediate credibility—even honor—and the notion that something so unmerited might come so easily left me both giddy and ashamed.

I'd not really been a praying person, except in public worship, but this city prodded me into the practice if only for want of companionship. My driver, I found out later, was Hutu. He tended to speak French. He knew so little English, and I so little French, that we didn't bother to try communicating. But he watched me from the rearview mirror with kindness in his eyes, along with obvious curiosity.

Out of the city, we climbed and climbed on a winding road—the only paved road that I saw, even in the city. I held a handkerchief over my face for more of the trip than I care to admit, and even after all of my vaccinations, feared unreasonably that the air might be filled with exotic viruses in combination with toxic chemicals that could kill me in a matter of hours.

The mountains were extraordinary, rising up as high as the Cascades of my youth, but without the snowy caps or jagged features. They looked like pictures I'd seen of Peru or of inland China, and the terraced farming up and down the slopes gave the scene unimaginable beauty.

And, again, the women. Always walking before us, ample derrieres dancing with every stride; backs arched and arms lean; necks strong under the enormous loads of vegetables, firewood, water, and unknown cargoes. They were, as I've said (and will continue to exclaim), extraordinary beings, like the most vintage forms of all creation.

We followed them up the mountains. I admit to regretting it every time we passed them by. They had so completely bewitched me in only three hours that I hoped to be greeted at our destination by a whole coven of them.

Chapter 2

THE SCHOOL APPEARED MORE like a compound, guarded by lush jungle and barbed-wire fences. The driver, whose name was Felicien, opened the gate, then drove us into a roundabout with an old fountain in the middle—beautiful only for its sense of longstanding prominence in the eyes of all who had seen it first upon entering these grounds.

As we parked, he took my scant luggage and led the way into the front entry of a modest building. I'd packed lightly, believing that most treasures worth keeping would be gained in the season to come. Other worthy treasures I'd lost long before boarding the plane—you, Donnie, being utmost.

The driver gestured for me to wait there while he stole away with my things. After a few moments, I was greeted by the kind of Rwandan woman who epitomizes, and then more, the beauty and dignity I've twice described.

"I am Prudence Nayinzira, the headmistress." She spoke with an accent that sounded so very African but greeted me with a warm smile and handshake that felt quite western. I loved the warmth of her large but feminine hand and looked up an inch or two into her large, interesting eyes. Eyes almost black, but somehow as warm as pastel. Perhaps the warmth came from the wide pupils that proved an unusually open regard for humans of every kind.

"I am Arthur Gilliam, your new English teacher."

"So I assumed," She replied. "Welcome to Africa."

"Is all of Africa this lovely?" I asked, referring to the world around us.

"Like your country, it is very diverse. Rwanda we call 'Paradise on Earth.' There is no place more enchanting."

"So I've seen. Have you been to America?"

"Yes," she said. "I did my undergraduate studies at Wheaton, and my graduate studies at the University of Chicago."

"Both great schools," I said. "Did you enjoy Chicago?"

"I enjoyed the people, and the deep-dish pizza."

We both laughed and I knew then that she'd be my friend.

She guided me out of the entry toward an interior courtyard—mostly dirt, with a large tree in the middle that reminded me of a Eucalyptus and might have even been one. The campus wrapped around that yard, with boys' and girls' dormitories on my left and right, and a multipurpose room straight before me. We glanced into the dorms—bunkrooms, really—eight beds times two, all made up precisely in simple bedding, each surrounded by keepsakes and pictures torn mostly from American or French magazines. The boys' walls were covered by typical photos of cars, sport figures, and women clad in swimsuits or tight-fitting outfits.

Noticing my gaze, my new friend commented, "I'm afraid that boys will be boys, Reverend."

"Of course, Ms. Nayinzira, but please call me Arthur."

"If you will call me Prudence."

The girls' dorm looked still neater, with some photos of robust young men adorning the walls with far more tame posters of flowers, animals and assorted accoutrements that will forever make female touches more refined and elegant than those of the ordinary man.

The multipurpose room served as classroom, cafeteria, game room and general meeting area. Round tables meticulously fastened to six points on the wall—four on the wall opposite the door and two on the wall behind and to the right as we entered. To the left was a door to the kitchen with some raised cupboard doors a few feet off the ground. To the right were two doors leading to male and female bathrooms. The floor was off-white tile, the walls of smooth plaster and the furniture made of composite wood with chrome undercarriages of the kind found in every classroom in America.

"All very impressive," I commented.

"Is it as you expected?" Prudence asked.

"Actually, a bit nicer. But is this the entire facility?"

"Well, the entry by which you came houses faculty quarters. And behind the multipurpose room, we have a garden. An unusual one, I might add."

The whole school was one small square, with a courtyard in the middle, a circular driveway with a fountain in front and a garden behind.

"May I see the garden?" I asked.

"Of course."

Prudence walked me into the kitchen where I saw lettuce heads, bananas, potatoes and more exotic produce stacked on a very clean floor. Two open fires kept a stew perpetually simmering. In concert with the stone ovens, I imagined this kitchen unchanged in a near-century of use.

A door beyond some counters led out onto the garden, which enthralled me from the moment I crossed the threshold. Even more than the larger compound, the garden was totally surrounded by thick stands of bamboo, grown more than twenty feet high. The garden ran the full length of the building, which meant that it was perhaps thirty feet wide. Bold, radiant flowers sprang up from the borders and rows of lush produce grew in immaculate beds rimming the most surprising feature of all—a swimming pool. About twelve by twenty feet, with a narrow cement border, it shone blue and clear and brilliant before me.

"Amazing," I said. "What a pleasant surprise."

"Indeed," said Prudence. "It is our little taste of luxury—our *coup de grace.* This was once a nunnery during the Belgian occupation, and they installed this pool for sanitary reasons; and perhaps for reasons of sanity."

"Are the students allowed to use it?"

"Yes, it is a privilege to swim here—one that is earned by the proper blend of effort and etiquette. They do not swim *en masse,* for they would certainly make too much noise and draw attention to the school, and to this unusual *accoutrement.*"

As she said words of French origin, she induced the deep gutturals of that romantic tongue in a manner that did the language great favor.

"Is it so important that we keep a low profile?" I asked.

"Yes. We have a few children of government officials attending here. And we represent an assortment of tribes. Occasionally, there is prejudice and violence against people groups, and the families of government types can unfortunately be used as persuasion."

I assumed she meant threats or kidnappings or worse, though it seemed such a distant thunder in this small Eden.

"There are rumblings of civil war," she continued. "I assume you've been told."

I nodded and noticed how furrowed her brow became and pondered the way in which a skirmish between parties and tribes might affect Prudence. I decided to wait on asking.

"Let me show you to your quarters," she said.

We walked back through the kitchen, through a corner of the cafeteria and out into the courtyard again.

"Where are the students?" I asked.

"Oh, they are on a rare excursion into the wider world. They have gone to Lake Kivu for the week. They won't return until tomorrow."

I remembered from studying the map that Lake Kivu bordered Zaire in the west. From what I'd read, it was a lovely mountain lake, large and teeming with fish. In fact, fish from the lake still provided a large part of the diet for a nation that survives mostly on subsistence farming.

"What a treat that must be," I said.

"Yes, this is their favorite week of the year."

"But you're not with them?"

"No, I stay with the school and let the teachers chaperone them. And the diocese provides most of the program at the conference center on the shore."

We reached my room, which looked and felt much like my dormitory room in college. A single bed took up much of the space, with a small desk and a modest wardrobe snugly fit. One ordinary window opened out to the courtyard. The only windows on the whole campus, I noted, faced inward to the courtyard. The windowless exterior gave the sense of a modest fortress, more than a campus. Later, I'd be thankful.

Prudence left me to unload my meager belongings and settle into my new abode. I placed a snapshot of my son—yes, Donnie, you went to Africa with me—above my desk. I lined up some books on the desk and ordered my clothing in the wardrobe and then piddled and paddled about for fear that Prudence would think me overeager to be with her. You might imagine that I was. She was lovely and smart and immeasurably intriguing, and I knew that I had so much to learn from her.

Chapter 3

"THE RPF IS ATTACKING from the north," said Prudence, as we ate stew and rice at one of the round tables she removed from the wall before I could offer to do this manly chore. "They are mostly refugees to Uganda, some Hutu, but mostly Tutsi. They speak mostly English, along with our Kinyarwanda tongue. Some have spent their whole lives outside Rwanda and now they have mounted a comeback, as you might say in the U.S."

"And who do they want to overthrow?" I asked.

"The RGF." She explained that the RPF was the "patriotic front," and that the RGF were "government forces." "There are many other political parties, some quite extreme, but these are the two primary influences," she went on. "President Habyarimana leads the RGF, which controls the army and the *Gendarmerie*. They are more paramilitary than American policemen and are not always to be trusted."

"When did President Habyarimana come into power?" I asked.

"In 1973, he led a *coup d' état* and became our dictator. He is Hutu but stopped many cruelties toward Tutsis that began under the regime of his predecessor."

"I thought that the Tutsis were the more affluent and empowered tribe." I remarked.

"Yes, in colonial times, because most say we look more European. Lighter skin. Thinner noses. Taller. The Belgians favored us with opportunities that only engendered hatred among the Hutus. But many Tutsis were driven away or killed."

"So, you are Tutsi," I said, though I had already presumed this by her stature and the hue of her skin.

"Yes. But right now, it is not safe to be Tutsi. If the RPF threatens to overthrow the government, some extremists might lash out at all Tutsis; even though the RPF has all kinds."

We talked more about politics until my mind was awash in befuddling names, initials and historical data. This I knew; peace was a veneer in Rwanda. This tiny, overpopulated country in the middle of Africa that most Americans knew nothing about now pulsed with latent turmoil. I felt less fear than curiosity, since I had so little to lose. But I did feel small, very white and quite overwhelmed.

I slept dreamily that night in convoluted images that smacked of *The Dark Continent,* which I'd reread prior to my journey. What was I doing in Rwanda?

When the children arrived the next day, the answer came swift and sure. They were marvelous. Handsome, bright and well-behaved, these Fruits of Paradise charmed me from that first moment until now.

First, their respect humbled me. They'd been taught a type of citizenship that honored their elders. Some had been discipled in a form of Christianity that placed obedience over independence. While the risks and vulnerabilities of that proneness became apparent over time, the first impression was one of teachability and promise.

They were also affectionate without smothering, curious without being annoying and enthusiastic without wanton excess. In short, they were a teacher's dream; which was handy, of course, since I had very little classroom experience and none, actually, in teaching English.

"Why, by the way," I asked of Prudence, "did you bring me here when you speak perfectly fluent English?"

"I didn't bring you here," she said.

"Then who did?" I asked.

"You don't know?"

I shrugged.

"God did," she said with certainty.

I tucked that revelation away and poured myself into this new vocation.

Most of the children, I quickly realized, spoke passable English. I disavowed the recommended primer in a matter of weeks and moved them mostly into literature. This was a welcome development, since fiction transported them beyond the seclusion of their little campus in their tiny nation, about the size of Maryland, and into the never-ending world of whimsy.

I chose *Tom Sawyer* and *Huckleberry Finn,* along with *The Wizard of Oz* and *The Diary of Anne Frank.* I sent my request to the diocese and was surprised that they delivered within weeks a box of thirty-five paperbound copies answering each request. In my naïve way, I hoped that books about the subtleties of racism and the atrocities of holocaust might be useful. As for Oz, it seemed like it would engage various ages in diverse ways and provide for the littlest ones the value of pure escapism. And, I knew, the book had more tones and currents than the movie.

It should be noted, Donnie, that I had pupils from seven to seventeen. Thirty-two in all, there were sixteen elementary age, eleven junior-high and five high schoolers. Of those, I assumed more than twenty to be Hutu, less than ten Tutsi and four Twa, who Americans know as Pygmies. Some students were orphans; most came from working class families; a few were offspring of government figures who sought for their children an education influenced by western notions of diversity and liberty. This school also afforded them obscurity—a small, remote site at the end of barely passable roads, in a province known for being relatively apolitical.

Donnie, you should know that I maintain the habit of protecting the precise location of that school to this very day, for fear that some reprisal might still be pending in a land forever poised for another wave of violence. No matter how unlikely it would seem if you walked among the Rwandans today. There is a peace and kindness about them, though not without a marked sadness, at how fresh their sufferings are and how wrenching the memories must be.

While the little ones delighted—and I'll tell you more about some of them in time—the student who most engaged me was a sixteen-year-old boy. Faustin is a common name in Rwanda, but this was no ordinary boy. A child of a mid-level government figure, Faustin stood about five-feet-nine, with a slender frame and defined muscles. His intelligent face questioned everything, sometimes with a shake of the head; not a negative, but an indicator that an explanation did not satisfy. He had great influence over other students, even the ones who were slightly older. When he chewed on hard feelings, his jaws rippled all the way down to his narrow chin and his dark complexion accented large, intense eyes.

And when Faustin smiled, the world jumped on its axis.

The fact that he withheld that smile until the most worthy moments created a will in me to earn such a response. Yes, Donnie, that impulse could feed into my *pleaser* tendencies, but with Faustin, I felt only myself—rather, my emerging self—and not the flimsy Gollum that I'd proven myself to be in the first two books that, I trust, you've read as preface to this.

I taught him English. And when he finished all three novels in a matter of days, we moved on to philosophy and politics. He asked me things during class that other students weren't ready to consider. He pleaded for more books on the Holocaust and I fed him Elie Weisel and some biographies. Once, during discussion of Anne Frank, Faustin stated without any accusation, "If not for American isolationism following World War I, Hitler and the Nazis could never have conquered Europe or exterminated millions of Jews. Am I not right?"

I had no compunction to defend America, but even less interest in simplifying something as monumentally evil as genocide.

"I'm sure that Hitler's rise went unabated, to some degree, because of American hesitancy to enter European conflict again. But there were other root causes—poverty, unemployment, a failed economy and certainly hateful ideologies—that fed into Hitler's hands."

"But wasn't Germany a most civilized nation? The theologies of the Christian faith are written in their tongue. We listen to their composers on BBC. Others copy Germans in every field, from philosophy to psychology. How could it happen there?" Faustin asked.

How could it happen anywhere, I wanted to counter?

Faustin became a true apprentice, you might say. So many questions and such eagerness to bleed out of me the kinds of facts and figuring that had always come easily to me. Of course, there were other truths and realities that I was not well-versed in. For those discoveries, Faustin and I would turn to a much better developed teacher. Prudence would change our lives—save them really.

Chapter 4

"Why haven't you asked me to lead chapel or teach religion?" I asked Prudence one day.

We were working in the garden with a small cadre of students. I pulled weeds as Prudence pruned and trimmed and exercised her expertise.

"Do you think I should?" she asked, with no trace of judgment in her tone.

I vanquished another patch of menacing invaders and managed to admit, "No."

"And why not?" she asked, with an air of mock incredulity.

"I don't know him well."

"Who don't you know?"

"Jesus." I said, almost whimpering his name.

"Have you read the gospels, man!" she said, almost in reproach, but in such a sing-song way that I nearly ran for my Bible.

"Of course."

"Then what's not to know?" she asked. Now she was incredulous, but the source of her emotion seemed more about God's knowability than my lack of knowing.

I paused and pulled a few more weeds out by the roots.

"I don't know him relationally."

"Well, do you pray, Arthur Gilliam?" She said 'Arthur' as 'Artur', which was her way.

"I pray."

"What do you pray?"

"Musings, I suppose. The things on my mind. But mostly to the Father."

"So, you think Jesus can't hear what you're saying," she both said and asked.

"I think he's dead."

"Well, sir, who in this entire God forsaken world told you that?"

I started to say, "Some German theologians," and then thought better of it.

"So, you don't believe in the resurrection, Reverend Gilliam." It was the first time she'd used that title since day one, and this time I sensed her derision.

"Well, I believe resurrection has been one of the most critical themes of Christianity since. . ."

"Oh, don't feed me that, Arthur. You think you can pull that—how did we say it in Chicago—mumbo jumbo on me?"

Now she softened and looked into me with a light so bright that it undid me. "Jesus is alive or we are all most to be pitied."

She started to walk away. She called together the pupils who'd been working near the distant wall of bamboo and marched them into the kitchen.

"Oh, by the way, Mr. Gilliam," as she referred to me around the students, "the pool is all yours for the next hour."

Up to this point, the indulgence of swimming had been reserved for the young people. I'd watched them come in threes and barely heard them swim with quiet exultation. This pool, you see, was such a luxury that the staff guarded the secret of it ferociously, perhaps for fear that intruders would get wind of it, or that neighbors might think askance of it in a world where so many went without clean water to drink. But here, students frolicked in silent ecstasy for monitored blocks of time and for specific points of merit.

Now, the pool was mine. And I'd certainly not earned it by denying the deity of Christ.

Oh, but swimming sounded good, Donnie. You've no idea what it is to adapt to the primitive ways of that continent, where every breath and bite can invite some unknown organism to maraud through the body. But I'd watched how earnestly they applied care to that pool and how schooled they were in the application of just the right chemicals, which were somehow shipped from a resort in coastal Kenya. This was the finest pool I've been in, before or since, and the context made it a splash of heaven.

I raced to my room to find a pair of shorts that seemed suitable. I'd, of course, neglected to bring real swim trousers to Rwanda.

I made my way back to the pool and stood on the side, looking into the clear and cool essence of it with a silent prayer of gratitude. "Thank you, God. No, thank you, Jesus."

And that day I began to talk to him. I supposed that if I kept talking, I might start believing that he was listening. And if he was listening, I might accept some post-crucifixion existence for this savior who'd been the subject of so many of my sermons and yet had eluded being the actual object of my faith.

The water washed over me, cool and vivifying. I swam underwater for a full length and thought of my sister for the first time in months, and of Lisa for the first time in days, and then I gasped with delight as I surfaced.

"Tell me how to understand the trinity," I'd been asked a dozen times by earnest God-seekers.

"Water helps me; good old H²O," I'd say, believing the viability of the parable, if not the alongside truth of it.

"God the Father is like water, the divine essence, in its obvious and best-known form. You can feel the Father and find refreshment from the Father, but you can't contain him in your hands; only scoops in our cupped hands, and even then he slips out between imperfectly fit fingers.

"Jesus," I'd continue, "Is like ice. Solid. Tangible. You can hold him, but not without being affected. He makes the mystical concrete for all the world to touch and be touched." Donnie, I knew this in theory all along.

"And the Holy Spirit," I'd say, "He is vapor and steam; mystery and fog. We have receptors to perceive his presence; we are receptacles to house his power; but we lack the better senses to understand or explain."

Oh, how I'd wowed them with this insight. Now, I was swimming in my own simile and still knowing not the power of it.

For that entire hour, I must have looked much like the children—mouth agape, eyes alight, splashing like a toddler in a bathtub. When my time ended, I prayed for another pool privilege to arrive quickly; and I found myself praying for the children. I prayed that this pool would wash their minds and strengthen their spirits; even heal them from the ailments of body and soul that might do them harm.

Then I dared to pray all of that for myself. And I prayed in the name of Jesus, choosing to say it with relish.

It wasn't an audible voice, but I sensed a word from the depths, bubbling up from that pool as it once asked another by the pool of Bethesda.

"Do you want to be well?"

However vaguely, I recognized that voice.

Chapter 5

"PEOPLE, WE SHALL TAKE roll today," said Mr. Karamira."

Roll call seemed silly, since we studied and ate and played and slept within yards of one another. Three weeks into my tenure, we'd not taken roll once. I knew all the names and all the students were present.

But the math and sciences instructor asked for roll in my hearing. I'd been lingering a few moments, gathering a few things, after finishing a lesson in English grammar. Now I lingered more.

"This time," said Mr. Karamira, I'd like you to tell us your tribe, as well."

Assuming that some worthwhile object lesson would follow, I watched and heard as trusting students stood when called, answering "Present," and then "Hutu" or "Tutsi" or "Twa." They did not seem demeaned by the moment, unless the Tutsi or Twa felt awkward for being minorities. Until the roll call came to Faustin.

"Faustin Bizimana."

"I am here, and I am Rwandan."

"Young man, I have asked for your tribe," said Mr. Karamira.

"Sir, I mean no disrespect to you, but I am Rwandan, as are these brothers and sisters here."

Faustin did not blink or flinch or blanch as Mr. Karamira's anger mounted.

"Young man, this order to take roll by tribe has come from the highest command of the Rwandan government. If you are Rwandan, you will tell me your tribe."

"Sir, you know my tribe."

"Then are you ashamed to say it out loud?" This was almost a shout.

"I am ashamed to participate in this roll call."

"Then you shall leave this room. Stand outside until I come for you." Mr. Karamira had regained his composure, but it did not suit him to be undermined by this influential student.

Faustin left the room.

When I'd gathered my things, finally, I tried to leave like the mouse that I was. Once outside, Faustin stopped me.

"Mr. Gilliam."

I turned and regarded Faustin, not sure if conversation would make me party to a student's insurrection and therefore disloyal to a faculty member.

"Mr. Gilliam," he said, "You know they did the same thing in Germany."

I felt a moment's nausea, and simply said, "Go on."

"They are sorting us out, sir. Just as the Nazis sorted out the Jews, and eventually the Jewish sympathizers."

I thought this to be both a sophisticated observation and a naïve correlation. Whatever motivated Mr. Karamira's roll call, surely there was no cause for assigning such malignant motives.

"It's astute of you," I said carefully, "to note the similarity. But you mustn't be concerned about that kind of distinction among tribe or creed in this school. We are a progressive school, with deeply held Christian values. Mr. Karamira must have his reasons, and perhaps they are being elucidated as we speak."

At that moment, the other teacher came through the door. Feeling out of place, I only nodded to him and walked away.

That evening after supper, I sat among colleagues in the multipurpose room, where the staff gathered to be social while students studied or played in their rooms. Mr. Karamira sat at a table with Prudence, along with our head cook, Miss Marianne.

Our history teacher, Mr. Claude Kanombe, sat at a nearby table, reading a book with his feet propped on a second chair.

I joined Prudence and the other two.

"I hope," I said to Mr. Karamira, "that I wasn't a bother to your class this morning."

"No, Mr. Gilliam," he said. "You were not."

"Though young Faustin seemed compelled to be so," I said, and watched a storm gather around pursed lips.

"Faustin?" interrupted Prudence. "What was he up to this morning? I love that boy."

I looked at Mr. Karamira, who seemed hesitant to answer. So, I started in with caution.

"He objected to an exercise, so Mr. Karamira allowed him to sit it out."

"What was his objection," asked Prudence, not finding my cursory answer enough to sate her curiosity.

"He simply took roll," said I, and then added in the most offhanded way possible, "with note of their tribal heritage."

I felt Mr. Karamira's glare burn into me as I watched Prudence turn in kind to Mr. Karamira. In fact, I had never seen her truly angered and was astounded by how much reproof she could impart using only her brow and her considerable eyes, now bulging beyond beauty toward fury.

Prudence stood, not leaving until Mr. Karamira would answer her glare with eye contact, and then walked with meaning out of the room.

I waited a few moments to allow my comrade to recover somewhat, and then I apologized.

"I hope I didn't touch a wrong nerve for either of you."

"It is not your concern, I assure you." said Mr. Karamira with a wide, eyeless smile.

Then he followed Prudence out the door.

Miss Marianne witnessed all of this with benign interest. When we sat alone, she started asking about America; our schools, cafeterias, menus and the like. I felt relieved to inform and entertain her with long dissertations on macaroni and cheese, tater tots and chicken-fried steak.

The next morning at English, Prudence surprised me by asking all faculty members to the start of my class at eight o'clock sharp. The students, as curious as I, sat up even straighter than usual and the teachers leaned on walls around them.

"It must be said," began Prudence, "that this school does not discriminate because of race or tribe. And even though we are a Christian school with religious curriculum, we are open to students of all faiths. While no one should be in any way hesitant to know and celebrate your tribal heritage, you will never again be asked to delineate it publicly. We are Rwandans."

Mr. Karamira looked at his shoes, I noticed. The other teachers seemed respectful but less affected.

"Thank you, teachers," she continued. "Mr. Gilliam, I apologize for delaying your important work."

Prudence and the other teachers left quietly. Faustin, sitting front and left, did not show any reaction at all.

After class, I found Prudence in the kitchen and asked permission to speak with her. She led me to the garden, beyond the pool.

"Did I create a problem with Mr. Karamira?" I asked.

"No, Mr. Gilliam," she answered. "The problem is as old as the human race." She paused, picking deadheads off the bougainvillea. "The sorting has begun."

"Surely you exaggerate."

"No, Mr. Gilliam. I refused to allow the faculty to follow a governmental mandate to hold this . . . roll call. But as you see, my authority only goes so far."

"So, Mr. Karamira is sympathetic to a governmental agenda? What agenda?"

"He is Hutu, as you might have surmised. Like so many others, especially in Kigali, old sentiments are being stirred up. Tired divisions and grudges are gathering wind. Lies. Hate."

"But not here. This is an island—a paradise," I said. "These kids love each other and behave so well. And the faculty is all so professional and educated—and Christian."

"Yes," she said. "But Mr. Gilliam, surely you know that there are Christians and then there are cultural Christians. Christianity has been the dominant faith of Rwanda for generations now. But don't you see it in America? The faith encounter of one generation becomes merely the forms and rituals of religion for the next? Religion will not stave off hatred. Sometimes, religion even causes hatred."

I'd seen this, of course, but not from the perspective of knowing eyes like hers.

"Are you afraid?" I asked in one of my most astute moments.

"I am terrified."

Chapter 6

THE SCHOOL YEAR PASSED without incidents notable enough to prompt an entry here. We taught the children, promoted them and sent some home for holiday. Then we spent those quiet weeks gardening, reading, getting better acquainted and listening to the radio.

In a country where few had televisions, the radio kept people entertained. But it did much more than that. In the hands of thoughtful commentators, the airwaves were a tool for good information. Stations like the BBC connected Rwandans—and me—to the happenings of the wider world.

Uprising in Somalia, with tragic consequences for United Nations peacekeepers. Something about war in Yugoslavia. In America, O. J. Simpson, a football player that I knew more from his rental car commercials, was indicted for killing his ex-wife and her friend.

And in Rwanda, a ceasefire of sorts. We heard stories of the RPF actually winning critical battles in the north over RGF forces, and then forcing a redistribution of power. The RPF major or general, Paul Kagame, grew into folk hero status. Growing up exiled to Uganda, Kagame rallied an army to return with the purpose of building a united Rwanda with broad ethnic and philosophical representation. But he couldn't do this alone. There were peacekeepers arriving from all over the world. Occasionally our staff would cross paths with soldiers flying the sky-blue colors of the United Nations. They came from Ghana, Fiji, Canada, Belgium, France, Nigeria, the Netherlands, Zimbabwe. Even Bangladesh had soldiers in Rwanda. The clear goal of the U.N. was to exercise international pressure to secure the establishment of democratic reform. Most of these soldiers looked so strong and projected extraordinary confidence as their SUVs roared past Rwandans pedaling bicycles and pulling carts. And the guns they carried made the Rwandan machetes look like toys. How could the U.N. fail?

An accord called the Arusha Peace Agreement was signed in August (1993) by various parties, but people around me voiced strong pessimism about the ability of all parties to live up to its ideals. From what we heard on the radio, even forming a transitional government snagged on every kind of barb.

I confess, my only conceptions of Africa before my arrival were rife with social unrest and political instability. Though I listened and learned, I accepted this turbulence as the norm—a continent no tamer than the lions and elephants I'd photographed on safari in the Maasai Mara.

I kept quiet except for some sympathetic questions and watched the consternation in the eyes of my fellows as they wondered about their country. And some about the safety of their families.

One night, we sat in the multipurpose room listening to the news. Debate broke out. Some in the room told troubling stories of rising ethnic prejudice against the Tutsis.

"And have you heard the RTLM lately?" asked Miss Marianne, the cook, referring to a partisan radio station. "Such flagrant propaganda against the Tutsis!" She said that last sentence with a glance toward Prudence. There seemed to be genuine concern in her eyes, but also an undisguisable interest in drama and intrigue, along with an acute awareness that Prudence was Tutsi.

"It is nothing," said Prudence. "Only talk among people with no real power and no real audience."

"It's not true," said Mr. Kanombe, the history teacher. He was a short, very dark man with exaggerated facial expressions and perfect posture. "People are listening. And they are believing too much of what they hear."

"Ah," said Prudence, "the United Nations will not let their evil rhetoric be turned into violence."

"But it is already happening," said Miss Marianne. "My cousins in Kigali tell stories of beatings and shameful acts against Tutsis. And there are so many independent militias forming. They're getting arms from the same countries that talk with such eloquence about peace at the United Nations. And what is Rwanda to them? We have no oil, no seaport, no exports."

Miss Marianne seemed to know a lot for a cook. I wondered about her story. Certainly, the fare that she served gave no evidence of much culinary training. But she was good to the students and sociable with the faculty.

"What is this RTLM?" I asked.

Miss Marianne turned the dial on the radio until there were shouts and rants and raves in both the Kinyarwanda and French languages. Of course, I was ignorant of both tongues and could only ask about the one word that I heard most frequently.

"What does *inyenzi* mean?"

"Cockroaches," said the historian. "These so-called commentators—what do Americans call them? Shock jocks? They refer to Tutsis as cockroaches."

"The government station is just as bad," said Miss Marianne. "They blame everything on the Tutsis and the RPF. And now that some rebel Tutsis in Burundi have overthrown the Hutu president, they're telling all who will listen that the same thing will happen in Rwanda unless the Tutsi problem is dealt with." She flicked her fingers in mock quotation marks as she said, "Tutsi problem."

I knew even less about Burundi than I'd known of Rwanda. But I knew Prudence, and her level head garnered my respect. She held her chin high and refused to be persuaded.

"The right voices will rise up. The right powers will succeed. God is in control."

And I chose to believe her.

But when classes resumed, I was surprised to hear that many of the boys had been invited to camp during the holiday. "It's only like your Boy Scouts," said Mr. Karamira when we heard stories about it together over lunch with teenagers. "They learn survival skills."

Still, it struck me as odd that only the boys I thought to be Hutu had been invited—including Faustin.

At the soonest private moment, I asked Faustin about it.

"It was only a boy's camp," Faustin said, evasive in every way.

"Why weren't the others invited? Your Tutsi friends?"

"It's a kind of training school for remembering our heritage."

I remembered Chinese Americans sending their kids to Chinese school for much the same reasons.

"So, may I ask? You are Hutu?"

Faustin barely nodded.

"And your experience at this camp?"

He shrugged, clearly conflicted, but trying to appear disinterested.

"Did you want to go?" I asked.

"My father asked me to."

"And what did you learn, may I ask?"

"You can ask, but it's really none of your business," he said, and for the first time a wall came up between us.

Then he softened.

"Mr. Gilliam, we learned survival skills. You never know what could happen, and we have to know how to survive."

Somehow, I didn't think Faustin had earned a merit badge in knot-tying or identifying edible foliage.

"Are you all right, son?" I asked.

Donnie, you should know that this was the first time I addressed anyone with the word "son" since you left. I hope you are not offended.

It apparently moved Faustin because he did the unthinkable. He began to cry. I held him, Donnie; that proud and bright young man. He cried on my shoulder and wept into his hands, and then ran away.

I knew not to follow.

I knew not what would follow.

Chapter 7

Not long after, some boys played soccer—football, as they know it. As was their custom, they played in the roundabout in front of the school. The girls frequented the inner courtyard, so this circle of earth was the boys' only playground, other than the pool. They devised ways to make good use of that circle. Since there was no room for two goals, and a circular space doesn't lend toward two, they used the fountain in the middle as the goal and defended it vigorously from all directions. Like a half court game of basketball, every change of possession meant that the team with the ball had to "take it back," or that's what Americans would call it. The boys used the phrase "clear it," in French or Kinyarwanda, of course. Clearing it involved kicking it against the shroud of thick bamboo that framed this curious playground like a stadium of waving fans, or against the windowless building, before being allowed to attack the goal. This "clearing" was like crossing a virtual midfield.

The ball was made of tightly wrapped banana leaves. It interested me that various well-wishers had sent real soccer balls to the school, where they gathered dust in a bin near the entryway. Perhaps the leather balls were too explosive and would fly too readily over the tops of the bamboo, forcing the players to go outside the gates to retrieve it; which required special permission. Or they might simply have preferred banana leaves.

As I watched that day, it was a furious match. Faustin showed as much acuity for athletics as he did for school, so he rallied one team toward victory. The other team stayed close, with Augustine providing most of the scoring. He was a tall, quiet boy, with fairer skin and a slight speech impediment. All the kids liked him, just as they admired Faustin.

At the critical swing in momentum, Faustin showed a bit too much aggression, sliding under Augustine to prevent an inevitable goal.

Again, the following happened in the Kinyarwanda tongue, so I report it imperfectly. But the tall boy, Augustine, objected, and gestured as if to pull out a colored card, which in soccer, I believe, is the equivalent to throwing the penalty flag in football.

Faustin erupted. He went nose to nose—rather, nose to chin with Augustine—and began to push him. I saw a flood of emotion break over its banks in a way I'd not seen or known. This was fury.

Other youth stepped between them, but not before Faustin uttered that word which I'd only recently come to know and despise.

Faustin called Augustine *inyenzi;* a cockroach.

Not being a fighter, Augustine slumped into submission and turned toward the door. Other youth tried to urge him back, but there was such a pained look on his face—no, the look spoke weariness, as if he'd tripped and fallen over the same exposed root so many times that he had not the energy to either dig and cut the thing out or bury it over. There appeared to be so much resignation in Augustine, as if this word *inyenzi* carried a power far greater than the mere assignation that pestilence insults normally carry. I remembered my brother saying, "You bug me!" I'd heard the terms *rat* and *vermin* and *snake* used in English, aimed in similar ways, but never with such force to injure.

I decided to intervene.

The other boys gave us some space as I walked Faustin to one corner of the building, where I could smell evidence of leach lines from our septic system. I chose silence.

After a time, he started in.

"It was a terrible call!"

More silence.

"He is not the referee," said Faustin, an ounce less animated.

A longer pause this time. Then came a rush of words and pictures that froze me to the core.

"We didn't learn merely survival skills at that camp. I lied to you and I am sorry. They taught us to use the machete. Where to strike. How to inflict the greatest harm. And how to be prepared for a summons."

"Faustin," I said, "who conducted this camp?"

He labored over his answer. Finally, he said, "Some RGF officers. And some *gendarmes*—you say police, right?"

I nodded.

"And the *Interhamwe*. Do you know them?"

I knew in part. They were young, extremist patriots who wore clown-like uniforms that draped them in the colors of the Rwandan flag.

"And what summons are they speaking of?" I asked.

"They talk of Tutsis overrunning Rwandans. Millions who've been in Uganda or Burundi or Zaire pouring over the borders and stealing the land from Hutus; killing and raping our mothers and sisters. They warn us about the RPF; that this is only a front for violent people who will enslave Hutus or cast us out of Rwanda."

"And the summons?"

Faustin paused again and I could surmise that his answer was only half true.

"They want us to be ready to defend ourselves when the Tutsis try to overrun the country."

This explained so much of Faustin's angst. He was a deep thinker and increasingly well-read, even in World War II history. He understood ethnic violence and its effects. Now, he was being indoctrinated in the strains of thought that he was learning to be wary of.

"How do you feel about all this?" I asked.

"Afraid."

"For your kin? Your tribe?"

"For our country. For my family."

"Do you believe the *Interhamwe*, and the others?"

"They say only what my father has been saying."

I knew that his father was a government figure, though I didn't know his politics. He'd visited once during my tenure. All smiles, with particular words of gratitude to me for awakening Faustin's interest in literature. He struck me as jovial, but with an undercurrent of fiery resolve that eked out in the character of his son.

"But Faustin, surely you've seen the U.N. peacekeepers. And you've heard and read about the new government that's being designed. Surely the Tutsis couldn't simply wrestle the country away from Hutus in front of the entire world."

"The United Nations has no authority here," said Faustin, as if playing back a tape from a powerful orator. "Their guns and trucks and helicopters cannot stop the tide."

His pupils constricted, his nose flared, and I wondered what spirit now possessed him.

"Why are you telling me this?" I asked.

His tension eased and the monster went back into his cave.

"Because you . . . because I . . . trust you."

"With what, son?"

His eyes flamed for a moment, as if to say, "Don't call me son. I already have a father!" But the fire disappeared in an instant and a kinder human being—a boy—said, "I don't know what to do."

"About the things they told you? About the things you're reading? You sound conflicted."

"I know who I am," said Faustin, with a childish harrumph.

"And so do I, Faustin. You are a bright, strong, thoughtful young man who has the potential to make the world a better place."

Donnie, I pause to ask your grace. I did not ever speak such words to you and should have. Often.

But, Donnie, there was something about Rwanda; in the lush landscape, or in the rhythms of the music, or the pulsating possibilities for either good or evil to take root and emerge and spread and hold the land like a stubborn stand of bamboo. And somehow, my own *becoming* presented hand-in-hand with that obscure little country; both of us crowded with regrets and unrealized impulses for the good, and yet capable of harm born out of the most overt face of niceness one can imagine. All of this, Donnie, made me say things I'd never said; *be* things I'd never *been*.

Donnie, my son, you also are a bright, strong, thoughtful man. And you've already bettered my world; likely, the world of many others. I should have said it sooner, but here you have it.

So how did Faustin answer? One small tear rolled down his left cheek, as I remember. He got up, walked directly to Augustine, and apologized.

They walked back to their peers, arm-in-arm, and the match resumed. Augustine's team won. They all behaved admirably thereafter.

Chapter 8

NOVEMBER RAINSTORMS KEPT THE pupils mostly indoors, which was as hard on the faculty as on the students. But oh, such rainstorms in a place where clouds hung low over mountain peaks and jungle-like foliage dripped and spilled its quantities of refreshment from the sky.

When the young ones were all in their rooms, the faculty and staff gathered. Even Mr. Felicien, the driver, guard, and all-purpose custodian, came inside rather than walking the grounds. Who, after all, would be out to do harm in such torrential rain?

We were actually playing. Prudence danced to some music on the radio, and others moved and made corollary sounds—we were the doo-wops, we might have said in America. And oh, Prudence was lovely. Her form, which I chose only to describe in part out of sheer respect, was perfection in motion. Tall, slender, amply curved, deftly proportioned and athletic in a feminine manner. I was entranced, but not in the sullied ways that marred my earlier narratives.

We were also laughing.

A special news report broke in on the music. A massacre in Nkumba to the north. Five sites. Men, women and children. Twenty-one in all. Others kidnapped to some horrible fate.

Miss Marianne switched to that awful radio station RTLM. They were already inflating the number of the dead and blaming the incident on RPF soldiers.

I saw Mr. Karamira transformed before me. Hook, line and sinker, he swallowed all of the exaggerations and speculations and began brooding.

"Inkotanyi," he said, with sarcasm licking his lips. I found out later that he'd referred to the RPF as "freedom fighters," but only in a derisive way.

Prudence turned off the radio. She turned and faced us all.

"The students must not be provoked by this story. Until we know the results of the investigation, we will not speculate. And when we do speak to them, we will do it together. Do we all understand?"

Heads nodded, though Mr. Karamira's only nodded down, so that his broodings were aimed at the floor.

Only the keenest could have foreseen the affects of this and similar stories. If the RPF was involved, then anti-reform elements had reason to dig in their heels, step up their rhetoric and pry away at the ever-widening ethnic divide. If the RGF or some independent paramilitary entity perpetrated this atrocity, then it made the cries for reform louder—and resistance to reform more covert and desperate.

To me, it was purely sad. But my observations of Mr. Karamira filled me with anticipation. What would he do?

The very next day, he told his students about the massacre. While this was not in my hearing, the aftermath took place before the entire faculty.

"Mr. Karamira, this is not the first time that you have directly ignored my instructions in the most provocative ways. I regret to tell you that this is grounds for dismissal. It is not my custom to do this in front of others. In fact, I've rarely had to remove anyone from employment. But this is an appropriate action and I feel it necessary to dismiss you from this position in front of others to protect us both."

Prudence stood to her full height and looked directly into Mr. Karamira's eyes.

Mr. Karamira seethed; standing, shifting his weight, sitting again. He could hardly spit out a word for the rage that churned from soul to stricken voice box.

Finally, he said, "You'll regret this. Believe me, you will regret this."

He stormed out of the room. Not long after, he left the premises, driven by Mr. Enoch.

"Do you know why Mr. Karamira left?" asked Faustin the next day.

"You will have to ask the headmistress," I said.

"She scares me," Faustin admitted, laughing a bit.

"Ms. Nayinzira? Why on earth? She's the noblest soul on earth."

"That's what scares me," he said. "She sees right through me."

"I understand. I'll allow that she's perceptive, to say the least."

"And very spiritual, wouldn't you say?" added Faustin.

"Very. She walks with Jesus," I said.

"I want to start walking with Jesus."

"So do I."

"You mean you don't? You are a reverend, I've been told."

"A bad one, yes." I found it liberating to be so confessional with Faustin, even though I felt vulnerable. "Jesus and I have been respectful acquaintances, but little more, I'm afraid."

Faustin nodded. After a few moments pause, he brightened up.

"Let's follow Jesus together!"

He made it sound like a bike ride or a road trip to Disneyland.

"Well, what do you mean?" I asked.

"You said, sir, that you want to walk with him. Is there a reason you can't?"

I thought of reciting a litany of reasons, but they all sounded inexplicable and indefensible in that moment.

"All right, Faustin. Let us follow Jesus."

I had a sensation come over me, both shrill and thrill that had a "no going back" quality to it. It was as if all I needed was a simple invitation from someone without guile or any agenda beyond companionship. That part—the companionship—was welcome.

I harkened back to the one weekend of my life when I felt competent in a sport. Back in college days, an excellent skier invited me and another novice to Mt. Bachelor in Oregon for three days of skiing. Once there, the expert deposited us at the beginner class on the bunny slope and proceeded to disappear until the end of the day.

But it was perfect. With another beginner beside me, we suffered the humiliations and exhilarations together, such that we improved to an intermediate level within days. I never skied thereafter, but wondered at how affective my friend's approach to teaching had been. Match us up with one other novice and let us prod each other toward adequacy.

We shook on our new agreement. Faustin smiled an enormous smile and said, "Shouldn't someone pray?"

"Won't you?" I pleaded.

"Dear God," he said, "and Jesus, Son of God, Mr. Gilliam and I have decided that the time has come to follow you. Lord, forgive our sins, teach us your ways and give us your spirit of strength to follow you forever. Today, we want to be Christians."

I blanched momentarily at the notion that I'd not been Christian before that day; but then I realized how purely true that confession was. In that moment, I owned it. That day, Donnie, November 20, 1993, is my spiritual birthday. And it is also the spiritual birthday of my little brother who is much like a son—Faustin Bizimana.

That very day, I asked permission to swim. Rains came and went during my hour in the water, but I could not be baptized enough or too much. I lay on my back, ears underwater, actively listening to the silence.

It reminded me of a trip to Israel that I'd taken in 1986. I toured with some students, pretending to lend expertise, and really only earned a free trip by volunteering to fill a bus with pilgrims. When we reached the wilderness of Zin, in the desert southland of Israel, I experienced a silence so profound that I thought, "No wonder Moses heard the voice of God." And for that afternoon, I actually believed that Moses had. Out of the silence came God's voice, and with so little interference, that Moses heard with clarity.

What did I hear from God as the rain bounced off of my upturned face and as my skinny frame barely held to the surface of an unlikely baptismal in the center of Africa?

Donnie, it's not so much what I heard, but rather what I felt. I was held. Held up. Held all around. Touched and massaged and propitiated and expiated. Without words, I was offered sonship and fellowship and a transforming friendship that made me a new person.

My son, I've written to you about the events of my life before Christ's coming. They were tragic and disappointing, but not without blessings. But I've also written of those days from a place of knowing, after Christ's intervention. You must know that I'm not the man I was and that Jesus has made all the difference.

Statements like that I once held suspect. They were the simple ravings of the sentimental ill-informed, fit for bumper stickers and refrigerator magnets. Now, they are my daily bread and they are enough because they are true. And it is so simple.

By the time my hour in the pool was through, I was saturated without feeling water-logged. As the waters held me, so I felt their buoyancy thereafter, even through the heaviest of days to come.

Chapter 9

OUR GROWTH SPURT BEGAN immediately. Faustin and I coaxed each other through the four gospels, the *Acts of the Apostles*, the epistles and even John's book of *Revelation*. We asked each other questions ranging from trivial to hefty and it all seemed to me as if I were reading the Bible for the first time.

Of course, aspects of my previous training came in handy to Faustin. And aspects of his ignorance came in handy to me. Both of us had been in church for much of our lives. We both had been, as Prudence rightly categorized, cultural Christians only; and from two very different cultures that had both found ways to marginalize Jesus to their own undoing.

To supplement our studies, we prayed through the *Psalms* and memorized favorite *Proverbs*. I'd brought Bonhoeffer and C. S. Lewis, intending to really read them. Now I truly did.

Faustin took particular interest, of course, in Dietrich Bonhoeffer. As a World War II hobbyist, Faustin struggled along with the German pastor's ultimate dilemma. Is it more evil to strike out at violent injustice with more violence, or is it more evil to allow violent injustice to proceed unabated?

When Faustin heard that Bonhoeffer participated in a nearly-successful plot to assassinate Hitler, his eyes danced at how practical theology could be and how credible this new hero was through his new eyes. And that tender young man almost wept when I told him that Bonhoeffer died for his convictions in a Nazi concentration camp.

"What would you have done?" Faustin asked as we lingered in the cafeteria over a very tasteless bowl of broth and vegetables.

"Only months ago, I would have been the type to keep my head down low. Oh, I might have preached against the injustices of the Third Reich, but at the first threat to my health or livelihood, I would have clammed up."

"And today?" he asked.

"I believe I would lay down my life. I'm convinced about everlasting life. I'm unafraid to die. I feel as if the principles and values of the Master are surging through me and could not go dormant in the face of a little danger."

"But how are you with pain?" he asked.

"Oh, untested I suppose." Then I thought otherwise. "Actually, I've known pain and it doesn't frighten me as it once did."

I paused, then asked, "You?"

Faustin smiled and shook his head. Again, not a no, but a signal that he didn't have all the facts yet. I realized then that the threat of death meant a much greater sacrifice for a young person. He'd not known love or sex, parenting or career. Laying down your life isn't as easy when life is all buds instead of already aging blooms.

But he was undaunted.

"I like to think that I would do the right thing. If the right thing is to turn the other cheek, I'd pray for the strength and grace to do it. And if circumstances made me choose violence as the better among evils, then God help us all. I would choose prayerfully and leave the judgment of my actions in the hands of the Almighty."

Wow. This kind of insight takes American Christians years to come by. We Americans are a slow-growth forest, spiritually. Desperation drives desire and most of us have so little of that. In Africa, where staples are not a given and freedom is hard-won every day, people look to God eagerly and grow at a rate that would stagger Westerners who believe we're smarter and prove otherwise by believing it.

Realize that Faustin knew the Kyarwanda, French and English languages and was pleading with me to start instruction in Hebrew, Greek and German so he could read the original text and German theologians in their own tongue. In Rwanda, common laborers are multi-lingual, giving even a casual visitor the sense that those sharp, resourceful people lack only opportunity to break out of cycles of poverty and violence. They are certainly not lacking in intellect.

You didn't need that speech, Donnie, but I must have needed to write it. My short season of life after Rwanda, back in the states, has left me cynical about Western brands of Christianity and far more impressed by the manner in which Jesus and the Way are saving and changing lives elsewhere.

Evidenced by Faustin.

I remember in seminary sitting with my coffee klatch pouring over all things theological. Inevitably, the hypothetical, "Would you die for Christ?" came up, along with "Would you denounce Christ with a gun pointed at your head?" Oh, you should have heard the coffee shop clatter of budding church leaders who might never once be persecuted for their faith, and whose primary physical threat would come from gluttony or obesity.

Or, in my case, a wife.

Since I had no real faith to hold up or to give away under the duress of your mommy's abuse, I can only say this: there was nothing remotely Christian about my handling of her. I did not turn the other cheek. I struck back by doing nothing, harming her terribly. Though something in me died during her attacks, I did not die for Christ. And though I did not denounce Jesus in the face of her onslaughts, I recused myself from following his ways. As you know, Donnie, I knew about Jesus, but knew him not.

Faustin knew the man. You should hear his prayers someday, Donnie. Not so much the words which are lovely indeed, but the level of honesty and intimacy. And it all came upon him in a few short months.

And here is the strange part. It came upon me as well. Not that I claim such great maturity then or now. But there came a kind of settledness with God, with truth (even the kind that indicts), with my past and with the future. Even my enemies, time would tell, were not to suffer hatred from me. And more than all things, there became this friendship with the Savior. Prayer became like breathing and yet more life-inducing. The Bible sang to me for the first time. Have you danced to the hymns hidden in *Philippians*? Or walked to the rhythm of the prophet's refrains? If I were married today, I'd treat the *Song of Songs* as a love manual and cherish my bride so heartily that even her sharpest flaws might be ground down into smooth refinement by the intensity of my devotion.

Oh, this is silly talk. Let me continue with the story.

Instead of telling Prudence, I decided to perform a test. In a sense, it was God whom I was testing. Could anyone really see a difference in my life while under the influence of fervent faith? I trusted Prudence to detect hypocrisy or mere ecstatic fluff.

It was December 28, 1993. I remember because we were all celebrating that day. RPF regiments were granted passage into Kigali to protect reformist interests, and they marched into the capitol amidst cheers and fanfare. They were conquerors, and many hoped they would be able architects of freedom.

Faculty and students drank Coca-Cola and ate a goulash of home-grown vegetables and chattered and hugged and gyrated with the best music on earth.

Prudence held me close, so tightly that I would have thought the wrong thoughts in days far behind. This time, I embraced her as a sister and saw her as God did—a radiant woman of God's own making. A work of art now so alive with hope and gratitude.

Suddenly, her lips were to my right ear, as if to speak sweet nothings. What she said was quite something.

"Welcome home, dear Arthur. We kill the fatted calf for you. We shod your feet and adorn your fingers and wrap you in a splendorous robe. For you were lost in a faraway place, and now you have been found. You were dead, my brother, but now you are alive."

I pulled away and looked at her. So completely out of character, I dragged her by the hand through the kitchen and out into the garden, to the edge of the pool where I took both of her hands in mine.

"How did you know?" I cried. "I need to know what tipped you off."

Without a moment's hesitation, she pushed me backward into the pool, laughing outrageously as I surfaced.

"It is the joy, Reverend Gilliam! I see the Father's joy! And that comes from knowing his Son."

Then she jumped into the pool after me. There we hooted and hollered until others heard. Gaining permission and confidence from the gall of the headmistress and the once-emotionally-constipated English teacher, others dove and flipped and flopped into the water until our exultations could not have gone unnoticed by friends, enemies or angels on high.

What a day. What a woman. What a life.

Chapter 10

THE POLITICAL SCENE DID not improve. Efforts at installing an interim, multi-partisan cabinet in January were intercepted by every bad influence. The ruling party wouldn't agree to contribute goodwill to a new regime without an amnesty provision. And since the atrocities of those rulers to that point had been so numerous and so ugly, the triumphant RPF would not allow a future in which past injustices would go unpunished. No amnesty.

The pre-existing authorities never quite relinquished power and the incoming government never quite attained power. That vacuum left all of Rwanda in a place so treacherous that even the international community could not right it.

Early appearances indicated that localized militias and paramilitary factions asserted themselves into the void. Over time, it became apparent that these factions were chanting the same verses and operating in pre-scribed chaos, choreographed by some hidden entity.

"There will be trouble," Prudence said to me as we rode with Felicien to gather supplies at markets ten miles from the school. "We must stock up with unusual quantities today. We will be stewards like Joseph; he saw the coming drought and rescued Egypt and his family."

"What will the trouble look like?" I asked, as if I were Pharaoh asking interpretations for a dream.

"Violence," she said. "Evil incarnate."

We'd heard more rumors of ethnic conflict. Tales of kidnappings found their way to our little paradise, where we wondered how much to make of it all. The radio told of grenade attacks on homes and businesses—Tutsi owned.

We'd received an unexpected visit from Faustin's father. He was all smiles, even as he suggested to Faustin that early graduation might be a good thing.

Faustin adamantly deflected, wanting to continue his academic and spiritual programs. His father looked worried and then drove off.

But this straight-forward declaration from Prudence made the notion of pending conflict seem more certain.

"You must go back to America," she said. "You will be safer there."

"Safer there?" I guffawed. "My life in America was wrought with vast dangers. I barely survived. This is where I found life. This is where I feel alive and safe."

"Your life and security are in Christ. America needs the Christ you love. Go back and be a great pastor."

"No," I told her. "I will not leave." I borrowed some resolve from Faustin, but mostly it rose out of a clear and strong leading from God. "This is where I belong. No matter what."

Prudence could not hide her relief. While she argued for me to leave out of a sense of altruism, she clearly felt better having me near; or even having another male body around, for what my slight frame was worth.

Meanwhile, the town pulsated with foreboding tensions. The marketplace already presented challenges for me. Somewhat the neat freak, I struggled with their unsanitary methods for fish and produce, the ever-present fly population and the knowledge of food-born illness in a place with such primitive practices. Honestly, I never complained about the boiling cauldron of weak and spiceless stew on the open fire of our kitchen, primarily because its perpetual boiling put my mind at ease—at least until the food hit the bowl.

But back to the village. Men stood in clusters, talking and gesturing in more animated terms than usual. Women hoisted larger loads onto their heads and kept their children closer at bay. Everyone seemed to be stocking up in case of crisis, and their caution caused shortages that made tempers flare.

Prudence, of course, suffered no shortage. Her demeanor and reputation earned the finest consideration from vendors, who always seemed to find "one more box" in a secure place.

The Interahamwe brought the most menacing element to that unusual scene. In their screaming uniforms and cartoonish *machismo* (there must be a word in Kinyarwanda for such behavior—Interahamwe, perhaps?), they always stood out and engendered the wary interest of others. But that day, they carried themselves with empowerment, stopping people to inspect their goods, cornering those who walked alone to harass them. A few *gendarmes* only watched, which had the obvious effect of emboldening the young thugs.

And oh, they noticed Prudence and me. Prudence would have been impossible to miss—tall, attractive and so clearly Tutsi. They took immediate interest in her. And me? They must have wanted to strut their feathers in front of the mild American.

But they only followed like ducks trailing a child with bread. Prudence has a presence that intimidates young men; a dignity of bearing that marshals mystical force. So they did not molest us in any way, and the more they tossed innuendo and threatened mischief, the greater was my sense that they were indeed children—merely boys starving for significance.

I found myself caring for them and wanting them to know that they were loved by the One who made them, and that God could remake them under Christ's influence.

Prudence held any compassion she might have felt close to the vest. We marched and then drove away without incident. But they called her by name, and one even said, "See you later," in a manner far too knowing.

When we reached the car, Prudence surprised me by saying, "Reverend Gilliam, isn't it glorious what's happening at the school?" She'd taken to calling me *reverend* since my conversion. She insinuated that becoming a Christian validated my ordination. Imagine.

And it was glorious. While a sinister tsunami gained momentum in the seas around us, a life-giving wave swept through the school. Faustin had become an extraordinary evangelist. Even before his transformation, Faustin carried great influence with the students. Now, his immersion into Christ's ways washed over others, as authentic encounters with Christ are prone to do. The same currents that drove his passion now tumbled and refined him to a fine sheen. Once a careful and strategic friend, now Faustin was generous and free with the gift. Once likely to use put-down humor to keep others in lesser standing, Faustin now chose words like a jeweler selects diamonds. His language took on a luster that made interacting with him, or merely listening to him, a memorable pleasure.

"Did you hear me?" asked Prudence.

"Glorious," I said.

"To see these young people take initiative for their own spiritual growth and health; it's unheard of."

"Unheard of," I said.

"You're not teasing me, are you, Reverend Gilliam?"

"Teasing?" I said, and the interplay reminded me of Lisa and a relationship that could have been so sweet under other influences.

"You know," said Prudence, "Easter is near and I thought the church should hear the student's stories." The entire school attended church a few miles away with some regularity, though we had a quiet presence to that point.

"Indeed," I said. "Why have you, or we, kept such a low profile at church and elsewhere through the years? I mean, this school is such a good thing and so many other young people could be served by knowing about it."

"That's a fair question, Arthur. I suppose that we'd grow. That's what happens with any really good thing once the word spreads. And we don't have room for many more, of course. And we'd have to hire more faculty. And then I'd find myself administrating a big institution instead of loving the children one by one."

She paused. Her brow grew a shadow.

"And this whole life of ours seems so fragile sometimes. I mean this, Arthur. You Americans claimed your freedom more than two-hundred years ago. Thinking in ways that are free—well, it's a birthright and a matter of habit. Here in Rwanda, we've had *coup* after dictatorship after massacre after civil war. We learn to capture small victories and treasure them, because we can't be sure of enough tomorrows to build bigger victories."

I looked into the eyes of this noble woman and saw sadness there. Usually, Prudence wore optimism as her garment and laughter with song as accessories. But the climate beyond the school dampened the high spirits within. I now saw that her exultation about the vivification of faith on campus was a crafty attempt to brighten her own mood.

"Prudence, your apprehensions are safe with me."

She laughed out loud.

"Are they, now? Why, you're but a baby Christian and now you're ready to be my counselor."

I saw the spark in her eye that told me she was toying with me. Then her brows pulled together to create a deeper crease on her forehead than I'd seen. We got out of the car and walked directly through the compound to the garden in back.

"If anything happens . . . if anyone comes . . . the children must go to the bamboo. It's dense and dark and . . . " She began to weep.

I held her.

Donnie, you must know how freeing it was to embrace a woman who could have been Miss Universe—if she ever had the unlikely impulse to enter such a contest—and still to feel only a brother's love welling up in me.

"They won't bother us, Prudence." I reassured her. "And if they do, we have the finest person in the world to guide us safely." Meaning her.

"But what if they come for me, Arthur? I'm asking you to watch out for the children."

"Oh, I would, Prudence. And others would. But you will be right here. And God is with us."

"You make me sick," she laughed. "You're starting to sound like me." I saw that her tears and vulnerability would be short-lived. I let her go and moved to a conversant distance.

"Why haven't you married, Prudence?" I asked.

"Where did that come from?" she asked.

"Friendship," I said.

"Well, then—friend—you should know that I am, or at least have been married."

Surprised, I asked, "What happened?"

"He beat me. He insulted me. He treated me the way his father treated his mother. Only, I didn't know. I didn't know before. He was educated, re-fined, usually gentle."

"What did you do?" I was more than curious.

"I told him after one month, 'If this doesn't stop, then I'm leaving you. I'll not divorce you, or love another. I love you even now. But you get help from Jesus or anywhere else you can find it, and you learn how to love me well; or you won't have arms long enough to hurt me.'"

"And?"

"He played nice for a few months, and then it all started again. So with the help of my pastor, I relocated. After a time, I ended up here. He has gone on with his life and now I don't have room for a man. Besides, God sent me *you*, Arthur Gilliam," and she laughed, and I laughed.

"Can you forgive him?" I interrupted.

"Forgive him? Oh, that came quickly, though my heart was sore for years over the lost relationship."

I pondered that notion and finally asked, "May I be so honest?" My heart raced.

"Of course, Arthur." Her face grew earnest and attentive.

"My wife . . . well . . . she had the same disposition as your husband. But without the gentle alter-ego."

"Oh, you poor, dear man," said Prudence. "And what did *you* do?"

"I let her hurt me. And I let her hurt our son."

"You have a son? And you haven't mentioned him?"

"I haven't believed that I deserve to mention him."

"Oh, let us fix that now."

Prudence placed both sides of my head in her hands with such forceful tenderness that I felt both loved and constrained by her vigor. She began to pray.

"Lord in heaven, this man has suffered at the hands of others; he's suffered his own frailty. Lord, God of grace and mercy, in the name of Jesus, set Arthur free from shame; free from any residue of bitterness. And Lord, set my brother free from regret; for the days ahead will require a strong man with eyes set firmly forward and head held high. Forgive what needs forgiving and heal what needs healing, and make your son, Reverend Arthur Gilliam, a warrior for Jesus."

Then she began to speak in a language unfamiliar to me. Not French. Not Kiyarwandan. I confess, my theology to that moment had dismissed tongues and most of the other miracles and so-called gifts. Unlike those who've relegated these matters to other epochs or dispensations, I'd rationalized it all under the heading "honest, ecstatic hullabaloo."

But in that moment, a surge of energy went through my being that at first tickled and then almost paralyzed and finally actualized into my deepest parts the content of that good woman's prayer. I felt free and forgiven; healed and blessedly forgetful.

Some new sense of confidence rose up in me and I stood taller from that moment on. My shoulders sat differently upon my torso. My chin in proper alignment with the earth had the humorous affect of bringing in my nose, which I'd always been overly conscious of, as it forever played drum major for my band of parts.

Donnie, I became a courageous man, and even a handsome one. In that moment. For that season. In that place. In her hands.

By God's grace.

In my newfound strength, I wept. No, Donnie, I bawled and blubbered and drained and laughed and grieved. I released a lifetime of practiced inhibition and unearthed scads of long-buried sorrows.

When the time seemed right, and my tears had drained the pool, she said, "Now tell me about this son of yours."

And I did, Donnie. With unbridled pleasure I told her about you.

Chapter 11

EASTER OF 1994 SHINES more radiantly than any holiday in my memory. First, there was my own newfound faith in the resurrected Christ. This alone might have made that Easter the best and brightest. More than that, it stands in sweet contrast to the bracken days to follow. The students presented a sunrise service in the garden and invited the whole community to attend. Dozens came. It was, to borrow Prudence's term, glorious.

It was a bold move by a student body that was hardly naïve to the brewing conflict in their country. They'd watched civil war through much of their childhoods, and now that the skirmish was supposedly over, they must have intuited more turmoil to come. No one would have blamed them for being backward and cynical. They were instead hopeful and courageous.

Some from the village answered an invitation to receive Christ that day. Others wept while children prayed for their souls and lamented their nation's woes.

Faustin preached. It must have been raw and probably lacked some homiletic precision and flow. Of course, it was also in Kiyarwanda, so how would I know? Faustin had only just begun to instruct me in his native tongue.

After Faustin spoke, the young people led a three-mile procession to the church, singing and dancing and waving banana branches as if it were Palm Sunday. Neighbors joined in. The Interahamwe marched along and mocked a little, but they were a silly sideshow. The service at church made so much sense, though I only recognized a few words.

When I reached my room at the end of the singing and feasting and dancing in strains and rhythms that my oh-so-Caucasian body never had known, I collapsed from rung-out joy.

I lay in bed conjuring up the songs of old Easters, inviting them to do a new work.

> *Love's redeeming work is done, Alleluia!*
> *Fought the fight, the battle won, Alleluia!*
> *Death in vain forbids Him rise, Alleluia!*
> *Christ has opened paradise, Alleluia!*

And,

> *Up from the grave He arose,*
> *With a mighty triumph o'er His foes;*
> *He arose a victor from the dark domain*
> *And He lives forever with His saints to reign.*
> *He arose! He arose! Hallelujah, Christ arose!*

Oft-sung and underappreciated hymns played back to me and spoke to previously uncharted regions of the heart.

> *In all the world around me*
> *I see His loving care,*
> *And though my heart grows weary*
> *I never will despair;*
> *I know that He is leading*
> *Through all the stormy blast,*
> *The day of His appearing*
> *Will come at last.*
> *He lives, He lives,*
> *Christ Jesus lives today. . .*

It was April 3, 1994.

On April 6th, at around 8:30 or 9:00, the radio reported a huge explosion at the Kigali airport. We assumed a bomb, or a crashed airliner. But we couldn't have guessed the greater story that would unfold hour by hour.

The thunderous explosion was the downing of a jetliner carrying President Habyarimana, as well as the president of Burundi and the Rwandan army's chief of staff.

Like much of the country, we all began to speculate. Was this the beginning of a *coup*, or just an awful, untimely accident? What would this do to the peace process and the plans for a new government? How would the mobs of Kigali react, and what evils could be stoked by the fires of irresponsible radio stations?

The horror began.

That hidden element that seemed to be choreographing various disruptions and atrocities now showed itself in all its malice. The radio stations were overtaken. The main roads into, out of, and around Kigali were blocked with zealous killers, and an horrendous *coup* of sorts took on arms and legs and machetes, with machine guns and grenades, as well. It's hard to call it a *coup,* since the previous and somewhat standing government took part *en masse.* But their insurgence yanked the rule of the nation out of the hands of moderates and the U.N. agenda. Even the Presidential Guard, the elite protectors of the government, played a central role in the awful days to come.

Once reserved for the extremist station, now the rhetoric of hate streamed over government radio. The message could not have been clearer, "Kill the *Inyenzi.* Kill the cockroaches. Kill the Tutsis. If your neighbor is Tutsi, kill him. If your nanny is Tutsi, kill her. If the children are *Inyenzi,* exterminate them."

By the next day, moderate politicians and civic leaders in Kigali were dead or on the run. Even Hutus who were sympathetic or protective of Tutsis were in grave danger. They were "traitors to the cause of Hutu survival."

The adults in our little community clung to the radio, while Felicien stood guard. We gave the students great freedom and only parcels of information; but Prudence began to lead us in some plans to either hide or flee. Our guard had a gun. We had garden tools for weapons. And we had nine Tutsi children to protect. And Prudence.

Over the next several days, the plague of ethnic cleansing spread outward from the capitol. Felicien came back from fact-finding excursions to tell us that homes were already being raided in the village nearby.

"There are bodies in the marketplace. People from our church. People who sold us goods. It makes no sense. It is craziness."

When we thanked him for gathering this information, a pained look came over his face.

"I must go," he said. "My son married a Tutsi woman. My grandchildren; they are Tutsi."

Though it terrified us to lose Felicien, we released him with warm embraces and best wishes. His final act was to privately hand me a gun and show me how to use it.

Mr. Kanombe, the history teacher, proved unhelpful in crisis. Agitated and talkative, he emanated fear around the young people, and we had to virtually quarantine him. Miss Marianne, the cook, continued to function, but cried every hour of every day.

On the fourth morning, the headmistress and I stood near the front gate.

"Prudence," I said, "you have to leave. There must be a way to get you to Lake Kiva. There are boats smuggling people to Zaire. Felicien told me. Or go to Uganda. Even if you can head north, Kagame's troops will protect you."

"I won't leave the children," said Prudence. I knew she meant it.

"Then you need to be prepared to hide with them."

She shook her head, but I knew she'd accepted the danger of facing a death squad. "What if we hide and they use the Hutu children to inform on us?" she asked. "What if those children are threatened and coerced?"

"That's my responsibility," said a strong male voice behind us. Faustin had crept out into the roundabout and stood ten feet away.

"Leave the students to me. I will bring them along. For the older ones, I'll persuade them how evil these killings are. For the little ones, I'll make a game of it. They will not betray you."

Then he looked at me. "Mr. Gilliam, it is you who must leave. This is our battle, not yours. Go to America. Tell the world what's happening here."

My reaction surprised me. A deep, firm conviction rose from my heart and I said, "No. This is where I belong."

They didn't argue.

Over the next three days, two sets of Tutsi parents came to receive their children. We surrounded them and prayed. To this day, I know nothing of their fate, which makes me assume the worst. Surely if they were alive, they would have returned to tell us.

Some Hutu parents came as well. They had apologetic looks on their faces as they took their children away, as if they were abandoning us to fates worse than death.

All the while, the voices of enmity screamed over the airwaves and we huddled together hoping that our remote little community would be forgotten.

On April 13, I saw the first Caucasian face I'd seen in months. A representative of the American consulate drove up to the gate, with a huge bodyguard from Togo. They began urging me to come with them.

"Reverend Gilliam, you must leave Rwanda. We've been flying expatriates out of Kigali for days now. You were hard to find."

"I can't leave."

"Sir," said the huge bodyguard, "you must understand. The *gendarmes* are a part of this. Schools have been attacked; students massacred. People have gone to churches for protection and thousands have been killed in those sanctuaries. People everywhere are on the move, and everywhere they go, they hit roadblocks of Interahamwe, who kill with pleasure.

"And ma'am," said the soldier, turning to Prudence, "if you are Tutsi, you must find shelter. You can come with us to Kigali. Ma'am," he said, choking on his words, "the women are being treated worst of all."

"Thank you, sir," said Prudence, "but I must stay with the children."

"Then God be with you," said the soldier.

"Reverend Gilliam?" said the American.

"I'm sorry. You came all this way at your own risk. But I belong here. Please find someone else to rescue. Please. Do."

As they drove away, chills came over me. But I turned to my new friend Jesus, and he bolstered my courage in moments.

"Prudence, we must prepare ourselves and our students."

We gathered the remaining staff and the older students. Faustin and Augustine were now adult in every way. They were brave, comforting of others and determined to save lives.

We showed the students to the deepest corner of the property, where the bamboo was old, thick and almost impassable. "This is where you must hide."

"And we must keep the little ones quiet," said Faustin. "That means that we must make it a hide-and-seek game, so that they don't cry." He outlined his plans and began from that moment to play hiding games with the children in other parts of the bamboo.

We began rationing food. We didn't even want to risk reminding the village of our existence by purchasing food. Fortunately, unlike the cities, we had well-water and a functional septic system, built by Westerners on short-term mission trips.

Miss Marianne cooked. Mr. Kanombe shivered with terror in his room, even though he was Hutu. Prudence and I guarded the compound. Faustin and Augustine became the teachers and caregivers and parents. We were twenty-seven students and four remaining staff, armed mostly with prayer.

Chapter 12

THE INTERAHAMWE CAME ON May 1st. They came at night. Later, I heard that they were deterred from coming in daylight, since a few Hutus with influence in the village believed it shameful to attack the school. But these now-seasoned murderers would not ultimately be denied this prize—Tutsi children and the thought of having their way with the considerable beauty who was the headmistress.

"You are not welcome here," I said with conviction from inside the gate.

They had not come quietly. This was not a stealthy invasion. They laughed and sang songs about exterminating insects. There were eleven of them.

"Mr. American," said one of their leaders, a lanky, laughing boy of nineteen at most. "Get out of our way, or you will enjoy the fate of the Tutsi *Inyenzi.*"

"There are no Tutsis here," I said. "Only sleeping Hutu children." I'd long since applied Bonhoeffer's ethic of relative evil to any necessary defense of these children. I lied without hesitation or remorse.

"We want Prudence," said an older man wearing the uniform of a policeman. "Send her out and we won't harm the children."

"Prudence went to her family a month ago," I said. "I am in charge here, and there is no one of interest to you."

"Then we will see for ourselves," said the *gendarme,* and he pointed his weapon at me. I don't know guns, so I'll call it a machine gun. And I don't know why they didn't kill me on the spot. Perhaps my unimposing build saved me, or else they feared the repercussions of harming an American. Or were there angels all around me, bending reality? If so, I wish they'd spared others and killed me. Or perhaps I don't wish that. I had a particular charge to keep and a flock to protect. God only knows why he allows some to suffer.

I'll say this, Donnie, with earnest faith, but not without some complaint. On this, the underside of the weaving of destiny, there are many loose strings and the design is less obvious and subject to grave scrutiny. I assume that God invites that scrutiny and, having suffered the death of a son under unjust influences, somehow empathizes. Still, how he can sit on his hands during genocide is beyond me. My theology is pure speculation, except in this: I have seen the heart of God and believe it to be good.

And I've seen evil.

The pseudo policeman shot the lock off of the chain. The crash of the gunshot must have tested Faustin's "game" to the limits, but when the mass of blood-mongers kicked through the doors and searched the school, they found twenty Hutu children sitting quietly in the multi-purpose room, with Miss Marianne and Mr. Kanombe.

"Where is your roster?" demanded the lanky member of the Interahamwe.

"I'll get it," I said, "but the Tutsi students left with their parents weeks ago."

I chose not to deny that we'd had Tutsi students, assuming that Mr. Karamira had already given an accurate accounting to whoever gathered such information.

They turned over desks and looked under beds and destroyed property. Finally, they headed for the back garden. I caught eyes with Faustin, who gave me a subtle look of confidence.

When the marauders saw the pool, they squealed like children. A few of them stripped off their clothes and jumped in. Others gave a cursory search of the garden, and even swept their machetes through a few patches of bamboo. But the revelry behind them proved too much. Even the policeman finally surrendered to temptation and dove, fully clothed, into the now-dirtied water.

They swam for hours. I saw them exchange what appeared to be drugs of some kind, and one produced a bottle of strong tonic.

Finally, they left in little bands of three or four, some assisting others in their drunkenness, some confiscating an item or two. All of them virtually forgetting why they'd come.

We waited a full hour thereafter and then relocked the gate, reorganized the school and invited the children—and Prudence—to come out of hiding. Some were sound asleep. All were calm. Augustine looked radiant with gratitude and valor. He embraced Faustin and the whole school entered into another quiet day of waiting and praying.

The greater distraction to prayer, at least optimistic prayer, became the odor. While our school was remote, as I've mentioned, there was no escaping the odor of burning and rotting flesh.

I'd known that smell only once. During my stay at Hood's Channel, the cabin that I called home suffered increasingly the odor of some dead thing. Assuming it to be a mouse, I took no immediate action. As the stench worsened, I called in the resident expert—Lisa. Seasoned by life in the relative wilds of that place, she suggested we look under the cabin. A crawl space allowed a vantage point from the wall on the seaward side of the house almost to the street-side wall. Near the far back, perhaps under the water heater, we saw a lump of fur. It did not move.

We took binoculars and looked again. There, lying dead under my house, was a fully-grown raccoon.

"Gross!" I said.

"Ah, it's no big deal," said the irascible Lisa. "Come on."

We changed into our grungiest clothes and gathered a hoe and a shovel. We began, then, to belly crawl from the seaward side of the house to the narrower crawl space of the street-ward side. As we crawled, the smell worsened until, looking down at the dirt under my own nose, I realized we were crawling in damp earth infested with maggots and oozing bits of innards. Waters flowed under the house, carrying the dilapidated corpse piece by piece toward the sea, with help from God's little cleanup crew.

I vomited on the spot.

Lisa began laughing and did not stop laughing until after she hooked the raccoon with the hoe, dragged it to the seawall, deposited it in a trash bag, stripped down to nothing, stuffed her clothes in the bag with the dead animal, walked across the road entirely naked (no cars came by—their loss), threw the remains into the ditch, ran straight to the seawall, and dove to the depths of the channel.

She finally surfaced, thirty yards out, holding onto a buoy. So slow was I that as she glanced back toward shore, I was still pulling off my stinking clothes. At last, I threw all but my underwear into the ditch and then followed her lead into the water.

When I reached the buoy, she said, "You really are a wimp, aren't you?"

"No argument." I said, still feeling the creep of death on my skin and tasting it in my mouth.

"Maybe that's why I feel so safe with you," she said.

"So you never want me to change?" I asked, half joking.

"I didn't say that," she said, and dunked my head under, where I accidentally took a swallow of seawater, making me reflexively revisit the remaining contents of my stomach.

"So sorry," she said, trying to mean it, and then burst out laughing still harder.

So the smell of rotting flesh brought back one laughable memory. Then, when I pondered the source of the reek, my smile disappeared. I felt a heaviness come over me. It wasn't like depressions I'd known where I despaired of finding myself and my purpose in life. This was the weight of caring; truly loving my neighbors and grieving the overwhelming sadness that had visited such beautiful people—both victims and victimizers.

We were cut off from the outside world, but reports flowed in by radio. Most channels carried horrid diatribes against the Tutsi and their sympathizers, but snippets came our way that told bits of the calamity around us. Hundreds of thousands were dead. U.N. forces almost nowhere to be seen. United States officials balked at another potential failed rescue like Somalia, while Americans watched O.J.'s ridiculous white Bronco crawling down the freeway.

"Arthur," said Prudence one morning, "our supplies are running low. Someone needs to go to the village."

I'd known this day would come, and I also realized that I was the safest candidate. Few expatriates had been harmed. Most protestant missionaries had gone home. Some *Medecins Sans Frontieres* continued to provide medical care around the country. Catholic priests and nuns from European nations did their hard work of blessing the living and the dead in a manner fairly unmolested. And there had been only a few attacks on peacekeeping forces, even in the most strained encounters.

"Should I go alone?" I asked.

"Take Faustin," said Prudence. "He can handle this. And so can you."

I nodded.

We made a hopeful list of foods and other necessities. I retrieved Faustin and we made our way to the gate. Reluctantly, I gave Augustine the gun and showed him its secrets in private. "God forbid you'll ever have to use it," I said.

The first mile of our trip was uneventful. I drove slowly, not wanting to kick up dust in our wake. At mile two, we saw our first bodies. Three once-amiable and helpful neighbors lay helter-skelter beside the road. Two wild dogs cloyed at the pale flesh, so that I felt compelled to stop and chase them away. I know that I only delayed their disgusting work, but it seemed right at the time.

I wanted to bury the dead but realized how ill-equipped we were for digging and how important it was to claim our supplies and return to the school.

Over the next two miles, I saw how useless my gestures were and would have been. Bodies of stricken townspeople lay stacked in piles, where animals without conscience followed the course of their instincts. As we neared the village, the only living souls we encountered would eye us carefully as they walked who knows where. At the entrance to the town, a roadblock of Interahamwe, a few *gendarmes* and other Hutus; one I recognized from Easter Sunday at the school, awaited us.

"Stop!" said one plainly clothed man with a machete.

I stopped and rolled down the window.

"Your papers."

Faustin and I both showed our papers. Immediately, two Interahamwe came around to the passenger side and asked Faustin to get out of the car.

Instinctively, I began to open my car door, but a man kicked it closed again.

"Where is Prudence?" three men asked Faustin, standing nose to nose with him.

"She is not at the school anymore," said Faustin.

The biggest man struck him with an open hand across the face. Faustin's eyes flared for an instant, but he quickly gathered himself.

"Where are the Tutsi children?"

"Their parents picked them up, after the plane crash," said Faustin.

Another man struck him with a fist and Faustin's nose gushed blood.

I felt as helpless as ever. No, that's not true. I'd felt helpless with your mother, Donnie, when she came after you. But this—what Faustin was doing and allowing—it was right. And in my new state of health, I would have done anything to rescue Faustin. But this trial was his to endure. My role was to pray. So I did pray as hard as ever I had at that moment.

And they let us through. Faustin got back into the car. We drove into the market. We purchased what supplies were available. On our return, they allowed us to pass.

"Are you all right?"

"Yes," said Faustin.

"You were so brave. I'm proud of you, in the best sense of the word."

"You would have done the same thing."

Yes, I thought, I would have.

Faustin never said a word about the incident in my hearing. When we reached the school, he cleaned himself up, changed his shirt and helped unload the car. Then, his face grew hard.

"We need a new plan. They will be back tonight."

Chapter 13

"WE MUST HIDE YOU better," said Faustin to Prudence and Augustine. "They'll cut down the bamboo or even burn it, to find you. They've run out of people to torment and they haven't run out of bloodlust."

"What do you suggest?" asked Prudence.

"We must act quickly," said Faustin. Then he led us on a bold and creative path.

In the multi-purpose room, we emptied out the crawl space that served partly as pantry for the kitchen and partly as a supply room for the classes. The foodstuffs and kitchen aids were stacked in front of the kitchen side wall in a way that camouflaged the existence of a closet opposite. The classroom materials were stowed in an attic space over the entryway to the school. Faustin pounded a hole in the upper wall separating the kitchen from the closet and covered the hole with a vent borrowed from a faraway corner of the building. This, he said, would allow the passage of food and refuse.

Then came the simple part of his plan. All of the tables were regularly hanging on the walls when not in use. He took two of the tables, hanging on the east and west walls, and replaced the hooks on equal and opposite spots on the north wall—one covering the entrance to the closet. To make the table flush, we stripped away the door frame. To discourage easy access, we added nails to all of the tables, top and bottom, to give them uniformity.

The only visual vulnerability was the brilliance of the paint where the tables east and west had been removed. We thought of dirtying the circles but couldn't make the ring go away. We toyed with painting the entire room but realized how suspicious that might seem in such a time.

We settled on an inadequate but simple approach. We borrowed pictures and posters from the students and stapled them to the wall, covering each pronounced circle with collages. They gave color to the room and appeared to be a legitimate enhancement to an otherwise institutional room; as long as no one pulled them off the wall.

Then we stocked the hidden closet with food, blankets, pillows, a flashlight and an awful bucket, just big enough to be useful and small enough to fit through the small hole to the kitchen.

We prayed together. When the sun went down, we said good night to our Tutsi brethren, including Prudence, and nailed the table over their hiding place.

We prayed more. We prayed that Faustin would be wrong about our potential visitors. We prayed, in case he was right, that our friends would be spared.

All of this, I should add, we did without the knowledge of the younger Hutu or Twa children, so that they wouldn't give away our friends accidentally or under duress.

Then we waited, Faustin and I at the gate, Mr. Kanombe in his room, and Miss Marianne just inside the front door to give an early warning if we were to signal her.

They came.

This was a surlier, more adult crowd; friends of the army officer from the village. Only a few silly-dressed Interahamwe this time; and they were subdued. The rest were fierce-looking men with guns and machetes. Seven of them in all.

"The children are sleeping," I said with quiet conviction as they reached the gate.

"Mr. American, you must deliver Miss Prudence or we will have our way with this school," said the leader from the roadblock, in a tone that lacked the hysteria of the first wave of invaders.

"I've told you; Ms. Nayinzira left long ago, after the plane crash, to be with family. I am in charge here."

"I know that woman. She would not leave these children."

"Then you know she would not abandon her family in a time like this." I deliberately avoided inflammatory phrases.

"Then you don't mind if we look around."

"Of course I mind," I said. "This is a school. Some of these children are orphans. All of them need their sleep. The Tutsi children have been taken away by their parents. We knew that we could not protect them."

"No one saw them leave," said the man, strangely reasonable.

"Do you think we would move them in daylight?"

"Perhaps I should punish you for conspiring with them," he said.

"I am not a Hutu, sir," I said calmly. "I have no political interests. We are all God's children. Punish me if you must, but I answer to a higher authority."

I'd heard or read that phrase somewhere and it seemed fitting. It appeared to take him aback. They started to leave.

Suddenly, he turned.

"I do not believe you, Mr. American. You are harboring enemies of our nation. Get out of our way, or I will shoot you."

I moved toward the door, my back to them. This time, a sharp machete or cutters of some kind cut through our chain. They moved past me quickly. Five went through the front door and two began hacking away at our bamboo perimeter.

"Please," I said, "let the children sleep."

The little ones were asleep; the older ones had been coached to pretend they were, and then to comfort and hush any little ones who might wake up.

They were meticulous. Every room, every closet, every attic, and every crawlspace was searched. Outside, the bamboo would not have been safe. With torches and flashlights, others from inside joined the original two and every square foot of yard and garden was laid bare.

"You have nine Tutsi students," said the leader, with frustration in his voice. His English was excellent.

"We *had* nine Tutsi students," I said. "I would show you the list, but I'm sure you have it already."

I should note that they searched the multi-purpose room with great care, along with the kitchen. The shape of the interior kitchen wall made it painfully obvious to me that it bordered a closet in the adjoining room; but something about the way we stacked food against that wall played a trick on the eye. Or else angels surrounded us and played a trick of their own.

Either way, the secret room went undetected, though more than one raider banged the wall with fist or machete handle, making sure they weren't hiding doors of some kind. They weren't of course.

As they prepared to leave, the three Interahamwe began speaking to the leader in the Kinyarwanda tongue. The leader turned to me.

"These young men wish to take advantage of your kind hospitality for a few days. Perhaps your faculty can teach them a thing or two. They are a bit out of control these days; no discipline at all."

He smiled broadly, insinuating a great deal.

"If I say no?" I asked.

"Then I will say yes," he answered, raising the nose of his gun.

"Then they stay," I said. "But I must continue to teach."

"So be it. Teach, Mr. American. But be careful. As I said, they are a feckless lot."

A *feckless lot?* How, I continue to ask, can highly educated people participate in atrocities like this nationwide massacre of innocent people? What is missing from their consciences, or what has been implanted, such that life loses its sanctity and violence its abhorrence?

The leader gave the three teenagers some parting commands in their native tongue and then left. I was relieved to see him go.

So were the Interahamwe. I recognized these youngsters and saw their faces light up. They pulled bottles of strong liquor from their backpacks and proceeded toward the swimming pool as if none of the rest of us were worthy of interest.

For three hours, they drank and swam and frolicked like frat rats, paying no attention to me or anyone. If we'd wanted to do them harm, we probably could have, but I saw nothing to be gained.

In the morning, they lay motionless on makeshift beds, passed out and snoring. They were pathetic *genocidaires,* I thought, and gave thanks for inept evildoers.

When they awoke around noon, Miss Marianne fed them and we all treated them like visitors from some other school, here to observe. Food stuffs were passed to the ones in hiding, and their bathroom bucket was emptied into the toilet while the intruders were applied elsewhere.

The young men swam and sunned for much of the day, asking for alcohol late in the afternoon. Since we had none, one youth left for a few hours, then came back bearing provisions for another night of revelry.

I felt so sorry for them. This was no way to live, and it might have been two of the most carefree days in their sorry existence. I found myself praying for them, even while I wished they'd go away.

Only one close call threatened our Tutsi friends. One of the young men, hung over and grouchy, came in for breakfast around noon on the third day of their visit.

"I want a table to eat at," he told Miss Marianne in Kinyarwanda. He pointed directly to the nearest one, the one guarding the closet and our friends.

Miss Marianne thought quickly, after a moment when her eyes grew to the size of golf balls.

"That one is broken," she said. "Let me get you this one."

She adjusted the nails on the second closest table, hoisted it off the wall, and pulled out the folding legs. When she flipped it onto its legs, I was pleased to see that the teen was satisfied.

Later, I quietly sabotaged the table that guarded our lair, so that we could prove that it was broken if put to the test again.

Around three o'clock, they simply walked out. No thanks or menacing remarks or gestures. It seemed as if they were mostly pleased to have been stationed at a lookout with decent food and a nice pool. I wondered if their testimony about "no unusual activities" would sway their seniors.

When all seemed safe, we pulled away the table and welcomed Prudence and the others out into the light. They were shaken, especially the smaller ones; but grateful. We all joined hands and prayed, thanking God and pleading for continued protection.

"How did you do?" I asked Prudence in a moment of privacy.

"I didn't sleep well."

"Nor did I."

"I was afraid that a littler one would cry or get sick. We used the flashlights only during the day, and we played games in hushed voices only when we were sure that no one was around."

"Prudence, you are a rare woman."

"You, Arthur, are a rare man," she said. "When this is over, you'll have quite a story to tell your American friends."

"Actually," I said, "I don't have many of those. I'd like to stay here."

"God knows," she said. "God only knows."

Chapter 14

"I'VE COME TO SEE MY SON."

It was June 13th. Faustin's father had charged up to the gate in a fancy government car. A hulk of a driver escorted him and a second vehicle with four soldiers parked nearby.

"Come in, Mr. Bizimana," I said. "What brings you here?" He wore a fine tailored suit and carried himself with even more confidence than I'd remembered. But this time there were no smiles, no affirmations, no affectations.

"I'm taking my son home to Kigali."

I opened the gate. The driver and three soldiers joined the politician as we all strode to the front door. I asked them to wait in the entry, while I went in search of Faustin.

Our prized human treasures were well hidden at the sound of cars on the road, and Faustin appeared as if by the sound of his father's voice.

"My son! How are you?" asked the father.

"My soul is well, Father, but my heart is broken."

The elder Bizimana seemed startled by such a thoughtful answer. He gave a questioning glance to his son.

Faustin answered with a question.

"Have you participated in these atrocities? I need to know."

"What atrocities?" said the father, "If you mean the safekeeping of our nation against foreign influences, then I have, Faustin. Soon we will be free and masters of our destiny."

"We, Father? Do you mean Hutus or Rwandans?"

"They are the same," said senior. "Any other view is treasonous."

"Then I am guilty of treason, Father. What will you do? Shoot me? Hack me to pieces?"

We were standing in the entry. I sensed that we might all benefit from a more comfortable setting.

"Please come in, gentlemen. Let us make you more at home. You've come all the way from the city." My hospitality had to appear thin, but I meant to ease the tension.

I ushered them into the courtyard where chairs sat under a small tree. I pulled two chairs away from the others so that the Bizimanas could talk. I started to walk away.

"No, Mr. Gilliam," said Faustin. "I want you to stay."

Mr. Bizimana frowned, but I pulled over a third chair and was pleased to notice that Mr. Kanombe, the fragile history teacher, had actually left the safety of his room to interact with the soldiers and driver. Miss Marianne served tea.

The following conversation was in French, the Bizimana family's favored tongue. Faustin filled me in on the content later.

"What is this about?" said Mr. Bizimana, looking first to Faustin, then to me, and back again.

"I won't come with you," said Faustin.

"What do you mean?"

"I won't be party to what you and your cronies have been doing. You're slaughtering innocent people. Women and children, Father. The elderly. What are you all thinking?"

"Inyenzi, Faustin, not innocent people."

"You sound like Adolf Hitler! You're a monster!"

At that remark, Mr. Bizimana turned to me and said in clear English, "What rubbish have you been filling his mind with?"

He then began to spew. Standing and pacing, he said, "Why did I agree with your mother to send you to this school. You've gone soft, just like I said you would."

Now I spoke. "Mr. Bizimana, I assure you that Faustin is a solid young man; strong, principled and a leader of our student body."

It happened so fast that I still can't believe it. Mr. Bizimana clenched his fist and hit me in the left eye, knocking me backward until the front of my chair held my knees and feet aloft and my head rested on the dry earth.

As I gathered my senses, I saw the strangest sight. Faustin stood behind his father with one arm wrapped around his throat and the other hand clasping his father's wrist, which Faustin pulled precariously high between his shoulder blades.

A soldier, meanwhile, aimed a pistol at Faustin's temple.

"Tell Mr. Gilliam you're sorry, father, and leave this place," said Faustin in an impossibly calm voice, "and I won't break your arm; or worse."

The soldier sweated profusely and shifted the gun from hand to hand, clearly befuddled by this unusual development.

"Now, Father!" said Faustin, pulling up on the arm almost to the breaking point.

"Mr. Gilliam," said the *genocidaire*, "my son has developed quite an attachment to you. For his sake, I offer my apologies."

"Accepted," I said, meaning it in full. Not for his wider crimes, of course. That matter was not mine to forgive. But I forgave the giver of my first genuine black eye. No, Donnie, that would be the second. Your mother. But I digress.

Faustin released his hold and spun his father around to face him. The soldier maintained his aim at Faustin's head.

"I have lost all respect for you," said Faustin, with only a tinge of anger. "I pray God's mercy for your soul."

"God's mercy," Mr. Bizimana laughed. "So that's it. Religious now, are you?"

"A follower of Christ," said Faustin. "And he loves the Tutsi as well as the Hutu."

Now Mr. Bizimana raged. "I could have this soldier shoot you! Do you know that?"

Faustin said, "Do it. To live is Christ and to die is gain."

"I cannot protect you if they come for you!"

"Who are *they*, Father? Your death squads? You are a coward. Do it yourself. Deliver me to my Savior. Do it!" said Faustin with force.

Mr. Bizimana curled his lip and fairly spat the words, "You are *not* my son."

He pulled the gun arm of the soldier down toward the ground and stomped out the door, through the gate and into his fancy car. The others followed. One, I should add, chuckling a bit at the evident superiority in character of son over father.

Faustin stood in one place until a sole tear dripped from his left eye.

"Are you all right?" I asked in time.

"I will be."

"Can I do anything?"

"Can you be my father?" he said, looking for a moment like the boy I first met.

"It would be my joy and privilege, son."

Faustin and I replayed the events to Prudence and Augustine, with input from Mr. Kanombe, who'd witnessed the greater part. We all laughed and cried and prayed together, counting it a privilege to know Christ even, to our small degree, in the fellowship of his sufferings. Prudence tended to my rapidly swelling eye and Mr. Kanombe retold his favorite part of the story; seeing my feet dangling in the air.

And we took turns holding and encouraging a young man, however brave, who had just sacrificed his own place among kin for the sake of friends, faith, and following Christ.

So, Donnie, you now know that you have one more sibling. The first, your half-sister, is yours by blood. This, your brother, is yours in principle. Though I can't force you to receive Faustin or to love him, I hope that this narrative will inspire you to respect him.

He is a man's man, Donnie. Like you, he made his own way when his first father failed him. Like you, he is smart and curious and self-contained, though he would claim that his confidence comes from Christ. Not knowing your disposition toward faith, I hope that you could say something similar.

I dream of the two of you meeting. God only knows, as Prudence would say. But I imagine that you would be friends. Two brilliant and resourceful men with so much to offer each other.

But if you choose to see all of this as the whimsy of an old man you once knew, I would not begrudge it.

As July neared, we heard reports of Kagame's forces sweeping across Rwanda. Government troops disintegrated, losing battles and morale. Many dropped their weapons and fled with the enormous *diaspora* to Zaire, where they would later instigate other terrible wars and bring about even more destruction upon innocent people; many in enormous refugee camps rife with illness and injustice.

But some extremists stayed in the fight and continued the pogrom against Tutsis, as if the near annihilation of a people group would compensate for the pending loss of their positions and influence.

Finally, Kagame and his troops did what the international community could not or would not do. They swept into Kigali on the fourth of July, establishing a kindred independence day for another nation. They found a city emptied of life and gutted of dignity, but their arrival opened the door for the return of sane governance.

They found imponderable piles of bodies stacked in the streets and floating in the rivers. They encountered evidence of the worst indecencies against women and children, who must have welcomed the relief of death. Some people died while hiding in outhouse holes. Others died of starvation and heat exhaustion in attics. Still others were maimed for life by machetes and somehow endured this holocaust in hiding.

There were many heroes; those who fed and housed Tutsis; many sympathetic Hutus who found it impossible to hate Tutsis and invented ways to preserve a few lives. And among the international community, some conscientious soldiers and diplomats risked their lives to stop the madness. Some gave their lives. Their efforts were little and late, compared to what might have been done, but they should feel some salve in knowing they didn't abandon all.

As for me, I did some good and not enough. If I'd known more ahead of time, or if I'd risked more in the midst of crisis, I might have saved more. It's impossible to resist analysis.

Certainly, one death could have been avoided. How I wish I'd been on my guard.

But as the RPF forces rolled into Kigali, and as the potential for reprieve seemed inevitable, I grew careless.

On July 3rd, Donnie. So very near the end. We almost failed the children.

Chapter 15

WITH FRESH REPORTS OF pending RPF victory, we started reveling too soon. We even allowed the children to swim; all of them laughing and singing. Yes, the Tutsi children were in the pool and Prudence was sunning in the garden. By God's grace, Mr. Kanombe had chosen to read in the roundabout for some privacy. It was he who heard voices coming toward the gate.

He ran screaming through the courtyard. "Visitors! Visitors!" It seems a ridiculous way to sound an alarm, but the tenor of his cry carried volumes of terror.

Somehow, a strategy found formation in an instant. "Augustine, Prudence, get the children tucked away," I whispered in a scream. They scrambled for their tiny compartment.

"Miss Marianne, it must look like you've been mopping the floor. Cover the footprints. The rest of you, keep playing and laughing.

I raced to the front gate, trusting that the others would play their parts.

When I reached the front door, an angry man was opening the lock—with a key? Four other men stood by, ready to follow him in. All of them carried machetes.

"Mr. Karamira," I said. "You are not looking to get your job back, are you?" I tried, believe it or not, to sound like Lisa—confrontative and disarming at the same time.

"Mr. Gilliam," said the castoff teacher. "Where is Ms. Nayinzira?"

"She left not long after you. She feared for her family."

"You lie," said Karamira with fury leaping across the roundabout. "We have come to express our regard."

"Then you'll be disappointed," I said. "She is not here."

Now they stood before me. I tried to look formidable on the porch, without picking a needless fight.

"Then we'll visit the children. There are a few in particular that we're very interested in seeing again." Evil smiles stole over their faces and I knew they meant to harm the Tutsis.

"The parents came for them," I said. "We have only Hutus here. And me."

"Lies!" screamed Karamira. "Let us through!"

I saw no choice in the moment but to let them into the building. I had no gun with me. If I had shown it now it may have only forced them to retreat and then they'd return with teems of Hutus to bombard the school.

Mr. Karamira's familiarity with the campus made him the greatest risk thus far. He trashed the office, pointed his henchmen toward the dormitories, and crossed the courtyard to the multipurpose room. I followed, not resisting or pestering, but praying and assessing.

Only Miss Marianne was in the big room, mopping a wet floor.

"Mr. Karamira," she said, feigning warmth.

He ignored her.

Seeing no students, he yelled, "Where are they?"

"The children are swimming. Can't you hear them?"

And they were, frolicking and laughing, playing Marco Polo, a game that transcends continents and oceans like Marco himself.

He rushed out through the kitchen and found the reduced student body splashing around under Faustin's supervision. Mr. Kanombe had retreated to his room. Better for us all, I thought.

Faustin stood and faced his least-favorite teacher. "Mr. Karamira. What brings you here?"

He did not and could not hide his distrust.

"I came to finish what we started," said Karamira. "You might not be a proud Hutu, but these children deserve to live and learn in an *inyendi*-free environment."

Like others, Karamira spoke to Faustin in French, but I pieced together his venomous words, then and later.

"They are not here," said Faustin. "You cannot visit your wickedness on them."

Mr. Karamira took a step toward Faustin, as if to strike him. But even unarmed, Faustin had taken on the form of one daunting young man. And he was the son of a government leader. The ex-teacher thought better of it.

He sent three men into the bamboo. While the trees would not have sheltered as well in daylight, they were still an obvious hiding place. They came back with their reports. No children. No headmistress.

All five stomped back into the kitchen and made a mess, without recognizing any signs of the Tutsis.

Finally, Karamira rallied them in the big room and prepared to make a speech. Faustin had followed us back inside and Miss Marianne leaned on her mop.

"This is a sorry excuse for a school; pandering to insects and teaching treason. I promise you this rebellion will not go unpun . . ."

I saw the recognition come over his face and my heart leaped. He stared at the collages, at the tables, and at the place where one table now covered an old supply closet.

An awful smile crept across his face and he began to walk toward the hiding place.

I was paralyzed. Unarmed and outnumbered, I couldn't fathom a solution or a defense. Faustin tensed up, ready to strike out, probably guaranteeing his own immediate death. Miss Marianne gasped in spite of herself.

"Mr. Karamira," said a voice from behind us.

Karamira stopped, not turning.

"Mr. Kanombe, what do you want?" said Karamira. "To spare yourself, perhaps? To beg mercy for consorting with rebels?"

"Turn around," said Mr. Kanombe.

Karamira began to laugh. "I don't take orders from you, you little man." He started walking again toward the table on the wall.

"I said turn around!" screamed Mr. Kanombe, and everyone turned to see him shaking profusely, with an unsteady gun aimed mostly at Karamira's heart.

Karamira saw it, too. "You wouldn't. You can't, Claude." using Kanombe's first name for the first time. "It's over," said Karamira. "You will be punished for harboring these enemies of the state."

"It *is* over," said Mr. Kanombe, his voice shrill with tension but made forceful by the weapon in his hands. "You are the enemies."

Then Kanombe shot Karamira in the shoulder. Before anyone could react, he shot again, piercing his former colleague's heart. Karamira's lifeless body lay on the floor, blood pooling.

The men with machetes obviously weren't soldiers. They did not react like fighting men and their interest in slicing schoolchildren to death must not have been too strong. They fled, with Mr. Kanombe holding a gun after them with spasmodic jitters. Faustin wrestled away the gun, chased the men out the door, and locked the gate behind them.

And we waited again.

The children came in from the pool after we'd taken the body outside and mopped the floor. The school held its breath in deathly silence for twenty-four hours, barely mustering the courage to deliver food and drink to our friends in hiding. We didn't even know how to string the little ones along without betraying our fear.

Cautiously, quietly, we turned on the radio to gather any information that could guide or comfort us.

A quiet hallelujah.

It was over. Kagame and the RPF controlled Kigali and the major roads. Perpetrators all over Rwanda were fleeing for the borders. Instigators were being rounded up.

We continued to show restraint for several days. Gratefully, our guard and driver, Felicien, reappeared at the gate. He'd lost his son and Tutsi daughter-in-law to a band of killers. His grandchildren—all four—were hacked to death in their sleep. Through his overwhelming grief, he described how the roads were safer, the food and supplies were flowing, and even Tutsis were resurfacing from every imaginable nook and cranny to find refuge with U.N. forces.

So, he and Faustin went out and found some U.N. Blue Berets and led them to the school. They turned the campus into a safe haven, and other Tutsis joined us. I became the innkeeper, caring and comforting and praying with people. I was their pastor and they trusted me.

Over many weeks, our guests filtered back into their villages. One by one, we released the students—the Hutus, with families—for an extended vacation. The seven Tutsi children stayed with us. Their parents never came for them, or even uncles or aunts or siblings. These were the new orphans of the horrific genocide of 1994. A few among immeasurable thousands.

That, then, became our focus. More orphans came our way. With help, we enlarged the facility and faculty. Prudence became an able headmistress of a large boarding school. I was the chaplain and English teacher. She let me teach religion and lead chapel services. I learned their languages.

Faustin came to America, financed by scholarships and what money I had. He studied at Prudence's alma mater—Wheaton. Sadly, his father was executed for crimes against humanity.

Augustine became a son to Prudence and schooled in Africa. Now both boys—men—live in Kigali. They are part of building a nation where no one is Hutu or Tutsi—only Rwandan.

Mr. Kanombe recovered from the trauma of shooting Mr. Karamira. He continues to teach history, with a special emphasis on holocaust and the history of genocide. He stands taller than before.

Miss Marianne cooks. Felicien drives and watches the gate, more like a parent than a guard.

By the way, I asked Prudence to marry me. I truly loved her like no other.

She held me in her arms and laughed.

"Arthur, the man I marry will be tall and strong; and he'll know how to sing and dance. He'll sweep me off my feet and make me dizzy with romance."

"That's not me?" I asked, smiling.

"Not yet," she said, "but you've come a long way."

Oh, Donnie, I had. I'd come a long way.

The first stroke hit my left side in 1998. The agency that hired me sent me home. Rather, they sent me away from my home, back to America.

I served churches for a few years—mostly interim pastorates. I believe I served them well. They loved me and respected me, and they heard the gospel with clarity and conviction. I left each congregation better than I found it. That seems a worthy legacy.

But my condition worsened.

I came to my current station in 2003, where they let me act as a resident chaplain until my speech center was affected.

This left me with memories of my exotic life in equatorial Rwanda—high in the mountains where gorillas still sit and strut, where bright people try to live away their memories, where noble women stand tall beneath their loads and where I was reborn and baptized.

I began to write. Not volumes; only three short stories. The first two are tragedies, with redeeming elements literally born out of them: you and your sister best of all. The third is a story of resurrection in the midst of catastrophic human depravity and loss. And it is a story of my second son.

Please understand me, Donnie.

I will forever be the lesser of two fathers who love you. Enough said; until we meet again.

God bless you and keep you; may God make his face to shine upon you and grant you peace.

Love,

Daddy

P.S. To the one who reads this manuscript; you will find contact information for my three children enclosed. Thank you for engaging them with discretion. These volumes are yours to steward.

CONCLUSION

Chapter 1

SHERRI LOUNGED ON THE couch, sipping a diet soda and reading a magazine. I stood in the doorway until she perceived my presence. She set her reading on her lap and sat up.

"Well?"

"I think I just met one of the most interesting pastors I've known."

I spent five minutes recounting Arthur's first and second volumes, and a full hour—with questions from Sherri—telling the tale from Rwanda.

"What do you need to do?"

"Contact his children, and soon, I guess. The guy's dying."

Donald Gilliam lived in Los Altos Hills, between San Jose and San Francisco. I soon learned that Los Altos Hills was probably the wealthiest community per household in the world. Donald, or Donnie, lived in a huge, gate-guarded estate. He made more than two hundred million dollars selling a Silicon Valley software company. He was married with no children. The telephone or email seemed the worst of all ways to approach the man. Now in his forties, he was certainly acquainted with the notion of receiving critical messages via the internet. But I wasn't used to passing them that way.

I flew to San Jose and rented a cheap car. The drive to Los Altos Hills took a half hour at most, and I felt my heart pick up its pace the closer I got to my destination. The neighborhood blew me away. Utter beauty and, unlike other Bay Area communities, nothing understated about it. Los Altos Hills was out there with its privilege. Every twist and tier meant bigger houses and more premier views of the South Bay.

Donald Gilliam's gate was decorative but tasteful. I rolled down my window and pushed a button on a console without any welcome or instructions.

"Yes," said a voice simply.

"I'd like to see Mr. Gilliam. I'm a friend of his father's."

The gate opened. I drove through immaculate gardens under an awning of giant eucalyptus trees. The smell was outrageous; like driving into a spa. The driveway ended at a large cobblestone turnaround—ironically, with a fountain in the middle. Since it wasn't completely evident where to park in the expanse of it, I found a place to angle my car and turned off the engine.

No freeway noise. No white noise of any kind. A few birds; a squirrel rustling in the bushes nearby. Other than that, quiet. I could hear my penny loafers on the cobblestone.

I rang the bell and heard nothing on the other side of the door—a large distressed-wood oak thing surrounded by some kind of nouveau tutor architecture. The trim colors were pea-soup green and burnt orange, both colors making an extraordinary comeback among the monied. Maybe others, too.

The door opened.

A young-looking man stood before me dressed in faded jeans and an In and Out Burger t-shirt. He was shorter even than Arthur, though not as slight in build as Arthur's self-description. Still, barefooted with hair tousled, he looked anything but formidable—more like the pool boy than a multi-millionaire; or the IT specialist on a house-call to fix the home theater system. With all of that data, I surmised that this was Arthur's son, Donald.

"Mr. Gilliam?" I asked.

"Yes. How can I help you?" His question had an intensity to it, as if the idea that I knew his dad had him piqued.

"I'm Luke Thomas. Your father is not well. But he's requested for me to speak with you."

"Come in," said the younger Gilliam, and I followed into an immense entryway with generous arched doorways to a formal living room on the right and a dining room on the left. Straight ahead, the family room opened up, huge and loaded with every modern amenity for work and entertainment.

As we passed in, the kitchen appeared on the left, spacious and modern, with two islands and the finest kitchenware. *Sherri would love to see this place,* I thought.

Beyond the family room was a sunroom with white wicker furniture, and Mrs. Gilliam seated with drinks already prepared for us.

Mrs. Gilliam stood and faced me as Donald introduced her.

"This is my wife, Jennifer."

Taller than Donald by inches and absolutely a stunner, she reminded me of an old lesson from my Silicon Valley days in a place where long-standing marriages were all too rare. "Men marry for beauty and women for money" said cynical voices, and this pair was living that proverbial dream. A grossly wealthy man and an outrageously beautiful woman.

But then he settled in next to her on a wicker loveseat and I could tell by their body language that they were friends and lovers.

"We're so curious," said Jennifer. "Where's Don's dad?"

"He's in San Diego. In a graduated care home. I'm afraid he's on his deathbed. Apparently, he's had a series of strokes that have . . . well, he's basically comatose."

"The last we heard, he was in Africa," said Donald; or Don.

"Yes," I said. "He was there for six years, until his first stroke. Then he served in stateside churches, and then at the retirement home as a chaplain. Then he couldn't do it anymore."

"Did you know him well?" asked Jennifer. However unresolved the father-son relationship had been, Don's wife was clearly interested and likely an advocate for full healing and restoration.

"No. Not until recently."

"So, he hasn't been in a coma for long?" she asked.

"Actually, yes, he has. But he wrote something when he still could."

I pulled three manila envelopes out of my briefcase and laid these copies of the original on a clear glass coffee table with white wicker casing.

"It's kind of a life story. But he wrote it to you, Don. I'm sorry if it sounds intrusive, but I read it; all of it. It's quite a story."

Don reached for the top one and pulled it out of the envelope. He read a paragraph or two.

"Is there something we're supposed to do?" he asked.

"Not really," I said. "He asks for your forgiveness several times; and for your understanding."

Don stiffened, as if I'd asked for his first-born son, or the patent on his latest technology.

"I'm the District Pastor down there. I'll visit your father and when he's gone, I'll plan a memorial service. He's earned a pretty good celebration, especially in the latter years."

"Here," said Don, "let me pay you for your services." He got up and headed toward a checkbook somewhere; but I detected an insult in his tone.

"Mr. Gilliam, I don't want any money. And I don't expect you to do a thing for me, or even for your father. I've read enough of your history together to know that it's complicated."

He stopped, sat back down, and held his wife's hand as if it were a life-preserver.

"That's an understatement," he said.

"I won't bother you more. May I ask permission to call you if your father passes away?"

"Of course," said Jennifer. "Please do. And Mr. Thomas . . ."

"Luke," I said.

"If we came, can he hear us? Would he understand?"

"Hard to say," I answered. "I've always been taught that many people can hear and comprehend when they're comatose. But I can't say, in this case. It's not a pretty sight, frankly. Oh, and I have more contact information. After you read this, you might want to speak to a few more folks."

"Thank you for coming," said Don Gilliam, standing up as if to dismiss me. "I appreciate what you've done."

This conversation was over.

Jennifer continued to exchange courtesies, until I started my car. A lovely, thoughtful woman. Even a Christian, I guessed. Which took me back again to my days in Los Gatos, a neighboring community. How many times I'd seen couples in the church, or in my office for pre-marital counseling, with a believing wife and a respectfully agnostic husband. Most of the men seemed very supportive of their wives' spirituality as a centering influence. But the men had a difficult time reconciling faith and science. Personally, I never quite understood that tension, since science so often suggests *how* but not *why*, and the Christian system tells *why* but not *how*. To me, biology and theology are worthy companions. For centuries, people thought so. But that's a risky worldview these days, both among those who are afraid to believe and those who are afraid not to. It's the fear itself that I don't get. But that's me.

I drove south to Los Gatos, visited a few old haunts, felt again some tired pains for things lost and gained, and went back to the airport for a quick flight home.

Mission accomplished.

Chapter 2

FLYING TO RWANDA SEEMED less practical, so I chose to contact Faustin Bizimana and Prudence Nayinzira by mail, and to invite them to contact me via email. It took two weeks, but Prudence wrote first, and Faustin within days.

While I didn't send the manuscripts, I did give a status update on Arthur's health and a brief description of the three volumes. I congratulated them on their accomplishments and thanked them for giving a dying man so many positive things to look back on.

Their correspondence indicated a great deal more interaction with Arthur than I'd imagined. He appeared to have written often until his impairment, and Faustin had even visited while in America.

I emailed back about my intention to contact them when Arthur died, and they in turn thanked me for providing care that they obviously couldn't.

Lisa and her daughter, Gretchen, presented the most complex challenge. This one seemed to call for a telephone conversation. The baby—girl actually—would be around seventeen. Lisa would likely be married. There might even be other kids. I didn't want to just show up. A letter felt too officious. An email too informal.

"Ms. Meyer?"

"Yes. Who's calling?"

"My name is Luke Thomas. I'm a pastor in San Diego. I'm a friend of Arthur Gilliam."

Absolute silence.

Finally, "How is Arthur?"

"Not well, physically. But very well, otherwise."

"Why didn't Arthur call me himself?"

"I'm sorry. He's quite ill. He probably won't live much longer."

More silence.

"What can I do?" she asked.

"Well, mostly, I think Arthur would want you, and your daughter, to know a few things."

"Such as?"

"That he finally grew quite close to Christ. That he found a legitimate place in ministry." My turn to pause. "And that he has always been deeply grateful for you. Your brief role in his life had a lasting impact." I know I was editorializing, but it seemed right to speak for a speechless man.

She sniffed, and I assume she wept.

I continued. "Your daughter must be almost eighteen by now."

"Yes, she just graduated."

"And she knows about Arthur?"

"Partly. But it sounds like you know the best parts," she lamented.

"I do. May I entrust a manuscript to you? Arthur has left memoirs."

"Absolutely. It would help fill in the picture for Gretchen."

"It would," I agreed. "But you'd have to read them first. They get pretty personal."

I made arrangements to send them, and she thanked me profusely.

"By the way, can I ask about your life? I confess, reading the memoirs made me very curious."

I found out that Lisa was married with three children, counting Gretchen. She lived in Seattle, counseled young women in crisis pregnancies, and ran marathons.

When I hung up, a great sense of satisfaction came over me. All of the interactions had gone as well as could be expected, though Donald was the wild card.

The Reverend Arthur Gilliam died three weeks later. No one but me ever came to visit, though Lisa called to inquire of his health before his death, and the Rwandans kept the email trail alive. He breathed his last in the middle of the night, in a small room, attended to by kind nurses.

I prepared for a memorial service in the smaller chapel at La Jolla Village Church. I gave two weeks notice to the family members around the world, even offering to pay expenses for the Rwandans. Then I drafted an attractive invitation to all the district pastors. I included a brief but glowing biography that hinted toward some intriguing revelations at the service. I knew that only a handful would come, but I wanted them to anticipate that it would be worth their time and effort. Finally, the La Jolla pastor, Phil Taylor, let me give a brief Sunday announcement to tease the congregation about a funeral coming in their own church. "You'll hear stories that will stir you to the soul," I said.

So, about eighty-five people arrived on a Monday afternoon. But not before family members started showing up.

First, the Rwandans. A tall, handsome, middle-aged woman cast a silhouette under the entry, on the arm of a taller man. As they approached down the center aisle, I thought at first that Prudence had found her romantic leading man. As they neared, I realized he was too young for her. This was surely Augustine, now close to thirty. He stood close to six foot three, with an amiable face and square shoulders. Prudence had perfect posture, olive skin, an enormous smile, generous lips and dancing eyes. Who wouldn't love this woman?

We greeted warmly and discussed the service. Both came with hopes of speaking a few descriptive words about the Arthur they knew.

"Faustin is still in the car," Prudence said. "He'll be in soon."

Within moments, Faustin arrived, showing the marks of strong emotion. He sidled up to Prudence and stood with her in a half-embrace. He looked five foot nine, with thick muscles, bowed legs, intense features and warm eyes.

"Reverend Thomas?" he said.

"Yes. Call me Luke. Faustin, I'm so sorry for your loss."

"Thank you. He was my spiritual father."

"I know. I don't mean to diminish that role, but he also loved you like a brother."

Faustin nodded, understanding the distinction.

Two females walked tentatively toward the front. I excused myself from the others and met Lisa and Gretchen halfway down the middle aisle.

Lisa walked like an athlete, with shapely, taut muscles and freckled, aging skin from too much sun exposure. She wore a little black dress that few forty- or fifty-somethings would dare to try.

"Lisa, you look exactly like Arthur described you," I said.

"Come on, it's been almost twenty years," she replied. "And I'm wearing clothes. You'd think I lived in a swimsuit, the way he described me. The pervert," she teased.

There it was already. That easy, edgy, transparent way that won Arthur's heart.

"This is my daughter, Gretchen."

Gretchen looked so much like her mom, but with narrower features like Arthur. Frankly, she was prettier than Lisa. She captured the best of both gene pools.

"Gretchen, I'm so happy to meet you," I said.

She looked me directly in the eye and reached out a hand. "Nice to meet you, Pastor."

"How does it feel for you to be here?" I asked.

"Weird," she said in age-appropriate terms. "But, like, I'm getting used to it."

"Sorry for your loss."

"Me, too," she said. "I wish I knew him."

"Did your *dad* come?" I asked, trying to respect the likelihood that much of her loyalty belonged to the man who helped raise her.

"He let mom and me do this without him. He figures, like, it was our thing, you know?"

I nodded. "Anything you want to say today? Either of you?"

"Not me," said Lisa. "I'd prefer to listen."

"Just one thing," said Gretchen. "I want to tell people that I'm his daughter, and that I'm proud of what he did in Africa."

"Cool," I said. "I'll let you know when."

The two from Seattle took a pew near the front. As if on cue, Don and Jennifer Gilliam came in. Jennifer also wore a little black dress, modest but becoming, and Don cleaned up well in an expensive power suit that made him look much more substantive.

Jennifer marched straight toward Prudence, who was still standing near the front pew. The two women exchanged so much information in a moment that they were embracing and crying before I could stage an introduction.

Don got side-tracked when he saw Lisa and Gretchen sitting on his right.

He stood before them, in the center aisle, bashful about approaching. Finally, he said to the teenager, "I think I'm your half brother. Are you Gretchen?"

She stood and looked him over cautiously. Then she gave a stifled teenage girl squeal and hugged him. Though Don was stiff, his flushed face told volumes about how much the moment meant to him.

Everyone met everyone. The rest of the crowd trickled in as the organ played familiar hymns. I followed standard form—scripture, welcome, prayer. And then I gave a fifteen-minute summary of Arthur Gilliam's life. His pained childhood in Oregon. The way the church became his safe place. His honors at school. Early ministries before God lit the flame of passion. And then I recapped Rwanda. More successful ministry stops, then illness and death.

Gretchen said her thing; brief and powerful.

Faustin spoke about their mutual commitment to Christ and how their growing faith buoyed them during terrible danger and stress. He was riveting.

Prudence took the pulpit. She wore a brown, Western-style dress, but with a colorful scarf that honored her heritage. In a strong voice, and in a beautiful accent that Arthur must have been too familiar with to mention, she said, "I met Artur Gullieme when he woss a small mon; small in stature; small in fait'; small in coorage. Den he met da Savior an' he grew. Artur grew in stature, in fait' an' in coorage He saved da children and he saved me, when he coulda been here in America with all you good people. If he coulda, he woulda saved more. If God required it, Artur woulda died to do it. I loved da mon. God be wit' you, Artur."

Lord, make me an instrument of your peace, I thought.

Then Donald's wife, Jennifer, said a prayer at her request, which I was thrilled to honor.

"Father God," she said, "receive Arthur Gilliam into his forever home. As this imperfect man has honored you so well in his final chapters, help us to honor his dying wishes. Give us the grace to forgive his mistakes. Give us the wisdom to remember what needs remembering and to forget what should be forgotten. Give us the love to receive each other as family. And give us the strength to live out our lives, from here on, with dignity and purpose."

"Amen," we all said together. What a prayer.

We sang once more; an Easter hymn. And then I watched, over coffee and cookies, as Arthur's three children made room in their hearts for each other.

Prudence and Lisa, Arthur's two such different loves, behaved like long-lost sisters, swapping memories and laughing away tears.

Jennifer, Donald's wife, took over my role—brokering relationships; with God and with each other. I released Arthur's family and friends to her and to God, knowing I'd likely not see them until the final reunion.

I greeted a few courteous parishioners, slapped backs with a pastor or two and made an inconspicuous exit.